THE HORN FELLOW

ff

DOMINIC COOPER

The Horn Fellow

faber and faber

LONDON · BOSTON

First published in 1987 by
Faber and Faber Limited
3 Queen Square London WC1N 3AU
Photoset by Parker Typesetting Service, Leicester
Printed in Great Britain by
Mackays of Chatham Ltd., Kent.

British Library Cataloguing in Publication Data

Cooper, Dominic
The horn fellow.
I. Title
823'.914[F]   PR6053.05463

ISBN 0-571-14614-7

for Ted,
who showed me the way;

for my good friends,
John the bowman
and Don;

and in honour and memory
of my father,
the best of men –

for all of them
with my heartfelt thanks

Let him who seeks continue until he find.
When he has found, he shall wonder.
When he has wondered, he shall reign.
When he has reigned, he shall rest.

Gospel according to the Hebrews

Resin smoke drove out, bursting. It thickened quickly and began to pillar up from the pine pyre.

An immensity of wing struck at it. And then another, ferocious, the patterned wingbacks, red and yellow, brightening up under a scutter of sunlight that fell out of a sudden wind in the trees.

The column was plaiting, brownness and purple, densening by moments, flexing, flattening and springing on wind turns. Sparked under, the gathered herb bed caught and reached up with billowing pungency at the beak and pebble-eyed head that fought and arched against the smoke.

Then there came cries, child cries, rage with fear and the knowledge of thongs. The wings opened again, man-length, the bright work on them there and gone in the toils of smoke; and the golden nape, twisting with the cries, flung back towards a thin blue memory that hung in remoteness above the rise of the herb-fattening heat.

Gradually, the great bird began to be taken by the fire.

The man stood forth from the trees and smiled.

'Good,' he said. 'It is good.'

He raised the horn to his mouth and aimed out over the trees to the valleys below.

The raucous voice spoke, succession growing with succession into power amid the countering of the hills. Call ran upon call, the notes peaking out and bottoming while steadily the small fists of cloud made on across the sun.

He smiled still as he played, eyes shut, blood-filled with light. There was measured strength in him: a strength of joy. He would play and play on till he no longer felt the draught of wings on his back.

'Still now! Be still!'

Knee-bent and strapped, Theuda felt the hand touch at his cheek. Another was pressing down with oakenness on his neck. Mud pushed against his forehead. It was full of all the chill of the forest deeps and his fear trembled with it.

About his head, there was leaf-mould and mosses and the knot scatterings of root and trunk, all with blackness and winter rot, so darkly that the lightness rose and kept rising in him, then fell away into swathings of heaviness.

He told himself that he must not lose hold; yet, foxwise, he chose to let be for a time, staying stun-still as if mastered though all the while poised and secretly eye-bright.

The forest air was webbed with the flarings of the horn, bright sounds from high out of a distance that bound in with water coilings and the work of wind in the topmost branches. Theuda let himself be covered by them, lay gaining his strength and then suddenly, carried by anger, flung himself upwards against the hand.

For a moment he was free. But his bonds caught at him. He heard a soft oath and then, as he struggled, a blow, heavy as iron, put him down again.

Later they said: 'Here, chew this. For your own good.' And then strong succulence, acrid and rib-veined, filled his mouth. He chewed idly at it, leaf and stem, dimly curious. Still dazed and pinned prone, he reached back at far-off, hidden things while above him they stood and talked in flat, covered voices.

Without measurement, horn and speech and water began to fold into one.

It felt to him as though his face were smiling. Bright winds flithered on it and the fall of sunlight and leaf shadows confused sense with hope so that he no longer cared over-much. He may even have laughed a bit when they drew him up and fitted the antlered mask and the bodyskin to him.

The horn was slowing, spilling over on to itself among the valleys.

Theuda stood. The antlers made his head sway. From the

darkness, he saw the two men, tall and daubed red and yellow about the polish of their heads. They held themselves apart, faces lowered from him.

The horn stopped. And of a sudden the air was heavy with ease.

'Go, holy one! Go!'

And with that the undergrowth took them.

He stood there, mouthing nothings into the darkness. Leaf juice seeped still in his throat. He stamped his feet and gave a laughing snort. His hands were tethered to the bodyskin so he beat at the air with his elbows. There were eddies and sluicings in his eyes. He would go, go somewhere and rest up . . .

'E – oh – e! E – oh – e!'

The shouts sprang up off the cliffs and fell away into the forest. But before they were crushed out altogether, other shouts and whistlings took up the cry.

Theuda twisted away and began to run. He loped along, following paths and damp black trails, any way that took him from the line of calls.

But it was quiet now. Wind and waterstream ran about him and the sun slid round his shoulders and back across the eyeholes of his head. All about, the approach of his passing drove up bursts of wings with piping and smacked clatterings so that he moved in a wheeling cloud of chaos and light.

Now he was running as if his legs had never known otherwise.

Once when the antlers caught in an overhang of branchwork, he stood there, snared, panting his fury into the sudden peace of the clearing. He had neither hands nor eyes and began to twist and thrash, blowing and kicking up earth. Finally freed, he paused and turned head high to sniff the air.

Shouts and calls rose again out of the forest.

Then the eddies came once more. About him, trees scattered, the ground's fall swelled and carried back and the grating of rooks was upon him yet away over the bounds.

His eyes rolled from darkness and back. Then once more he was gone.

Fear still filled him with its utterness, pricked him on to run; but in with this was an abundance of laughter that stripped consequence from all, from everything. Thorns would snatch at him, boughs massively bar against arm or leg: yet for him there seemed nothing in this, as if the pain of it were not even his.

He came breaking from the thickets, running topwise down a bank of sprung grass to where a stream lay fierce among the rocks. By its edge he steadied himself and peered sunwards up into the disarrayment of the towering woods. The stream's drive and the thick purling of the waterfall behind him formed a seamless closure of sound.

The sun was falling.

He shook his head and blinked.

Did he have to run on? The warm lightness within him was whispering that they had gone now, the shouters . . .

Pah!

In loathing, he turned and spat the sodden green pad into the stream. Then, crouching, he sucked water through the mask and swilled out his mouth.

Though he was quite still now and had all his balance yet it was as if there were nothing fixed in the form of things about him. He saw all of it with precision but could not find a pattern, beech and earth and dark water. The antlered head rocked upon the sky: the animal heat of anger was once again flushing up against the binding of the bodyskin.

Then dimly, beyond his fury, he sensed a tautening within himself. And even as he did so, a prick of sunlight on metal struck at his eye from the higher wood. He just saw it and spun, taking to the air, stamping up off the rock in a half-formed bound of fear.

A cord of fire caught him across the shoulders and went clattering away among the rocks. He twisted at it with a grunt and his flight was turned so that he came splayfoot down on

4

slitheriness. He went off it backwards and sprawled hard on the polished surge of water as it ran into the channel above the fall. A mere moment later, as he breached up to pluck air from the day, he was sucked over the lip of the force, a bundle of limb and antler as ungainly as the flood-drawn branch of a tree.

Even in the noise of the drop, there sparked brightly in his mind: No! not just for this . . . ! But with that he was gone and the great-mouthed pillar force had driven him to the depths.

No!

And with all the strong agility of fear and belief, he kicked. Bubbles were netting about his face, golden in the peat dark-ness. Somewhere above waited the light.

And again: No!

And with it, he kicked again though less strongly now for somehow water had plunged icily into the flaming fist of his chest. The daylight remembered and the half of a life passed became part of the thundering cavern about him.

No! he urged once more and then the waters broke and, spewing, he bit furiously into the warmth.

In the hunger of that moment, Theuda glimpsed the gorge below. Shadows hung there among sharp-coloured mosses and all the moulder of waterlogged trees. Then he sank again: but was striving sideways across the current, thrusting him-self off the bed with violence. When next he rose, dismay seized him for he saw himself close to the gorge mouth. There cream waters boiled; and lower beyond, ominously, a great mizzle of spray hung fine, brightened in the sinking sun.

'No!' he cried, this time aloud; and, screwing round, drove his head at the rocks. He lashed with leg and bucked his head, searching. Then, just as he felt himself being drawn into the gathering speed, his antlerwork lodged itself between two boulders. He held, not daring to try more. Then, braced on his neck, he managed to ease up his legs and slowly pull round to hang gasping in the backwater.

5

Later, when he had landed himself and gone to cover, he found a sharp rock to cut away the thongs. He rid himself of the mask and the pale skin and pushed them down into a quaggy patch under the cliffs.

He stood up and peered round through the trees. A bird, loud with piping, fled hugging the bloom on the pool. Theuda smiled and breathed in slowly, eyes closed and head back, drawing round his shoulders to feel how the arrow had hurt him.

He climbed a bit and tucked himself into a notch of the cliff where cushion grass grew thick in the sun. The air was still and surrounded by the sound of the falls.

Just till dusk . . ., he thought and lay back.

There was still the folding and floating in him: so that when he stared far out into the depths of the blue, the call of a bird with the water noises was all of a oneness with him and yet clearly detached. But now there was no great matter in this and of a sudden Theuda found himself laughing and then laughing more so that his long face creased and his eyes opened up. And it kept growing within him, the laughing, so that soon it reverberated out of all his being as if it would carry him with it into the beyond.

And then – so cleanly that it cut into his awareness as a blade might into a heart – the tumult of his happiness stilled from its bounding vastness into a simple breath of peace and he slept.

He moved under moonlight, his body crazed all over by branches of pitch.

Away from the stream, the spring forest opened; and here, among the massive, waxen columns, he walked with a sureness of ease, his soles picking safety on moss and sharp grass. His way was always upwards for he sought the freedom of seclusion for the night. He felt the animals close by as he passed and occasionally the stillness would move in alarm: otherwise he climbed alone.

The shouts had continued to ring up in the air till shortly

after sunfall. Then the horn had sounded again – close or far, somewhere in the interlocking of the hills – one solemn soaring that descended quickly into the shadows of the valleys' dusk. Theuda had stopped, heart-held, till long after the call had been swallowed up by the air. From then on into the early darkness, nothing. He climbed now only for his own content.

He fell asleep high on the hill, clutching his tunic of hide about him for the spring was still young and the nights of the north hung long on the edge of winter. Waist-deep in a bank of old leaves he lay, there at the foot of a ridge that topped the angle of the clearing. Owls and foxes were on the move and, far away to the west, wolves were out; but he heard little of this in his exhaustion and was long asleep when the moon fell on to the forest spears and true darkness took the leaf bed.

Whssssht!

At the sound, Theuda went bounding up in a cloud of leaves even before he fully awoke. Only from the safety of the trees did he turn and look.

The man was frowning at him. Short and built of strength and balance, his eyes saw like a hawk's. His hair flamed and across his back lay a bow and its arrows. There was nothing of fear in him: only puzzlement.

'I woke you,' he said. Theuda waited. 'You have a name?'

The sun began to rise.

'I am Theuda, son of Algar, himself a son of Hoel, men of no small standing. We claim kinship with . . .'

'These are men's names,' broke in the other. 'What of the woman who bore you?'

Theuda looked at him.

'My mother was called Aldith.' He paused. 'And you?'

'My mother was Moolde. I am Deor.'

Theuda shook his head. The sleep had gone now; and with the growth of light, a new feeling came into him. He began to speak:

All-seeing, the falcon of hope.
Mountain and field alike
With her fire, she will cross.
Menfolk must follow:
It is her or a death.
Winds rally,
Storms are her plumage:
The rat of fear
Lies low in the grass.

His mouth emptied itself and closed. He gazed with a momentary arrogance into the sky and then scratched his buttock.

'You are a wordspeaker,' said Deor.

'No,' answered Theuda. 'That was not me speaking.'

Large birds of dun colouring flew weightily across the clearing. In the valley below, honeyed daylight was spreading.

Deor asked Theuda if he had slept the night long on the leaf bed.

'All of a chill night,' replied Theuda.

Deor straightened up. They met by the leaves.

'Truly? Then it is a mishap you have brought on yourself. Last night was a spirit night.' He gestured up towards a great spike of a stone which stood on the ridge. 'To sleep near the stone on such a night may well make a man die. If not, then for certain he will either fall mad or become a wordspeaker.'

Theuda stared at himself.

'Have you come far for this?' Deor's voice was low.

'Far? Yes, I have travelled long ways.' He glanced at Deor and saw the man's eyes holding him fixed. He could scarcely look at it.

'Things must be,' said Deor. 'There is no joy in hating them for it.'

'Indeed,' replied Theuda.

They walked together down to the clearing's foot where the sunlight was starting to pool.

'Your back . . .' said Deor of a sudden.

Theuda made as if he had not heard and walked on, seeking to step out of a memory.

But Deor had stopped.

'You – it was you yesterday!'

'I don't remember,' said Theuda swiftly.

Deor was down on his knee, head bent.

'When the Willowmonth Sorel is not taken then grief comes for sure. But the Sorel himself will know joy for he is then free and untouchable. Go,' he said, 'you are hallowed. It is for you to live.'

Theuda was angry.

'Go?' he burst out and drew Deor up by the shoulder. 'I am come here and shall stay. This I say to you.'

Deor looked at him and slowly a smile ran into his eyes.

'Then, Lord Sorel,' he said with a laugh, 'so am I your companion in blood. For it was I who touched you yesterday.'

2

He still knew it, knew it for certain. Yet, in spite of this, he was quite without any real understanding of it.

The Willowmonth days pressed on. Spooning and spray-light, showers drove here and there. Cubs came; and out in the forest cloudlike structures of bells hung caught on the banks among the ribwork of the great roots.

Theuda's life was alone. Till the month's end, he must stay apart – that was the word of Deor's people. He had a hut eastward round the hill from them and it was as if he had been reviled. He found food on the flat rock beyond the beech and each day he took it though never once did he see it brought. He filled the hours of light caught between restlessness and sleep, still overwhelmed by the sureness but stifled by an impatience to reach understanding.

No longer did he dream the dream; and in that too there was pain. Once though, travelling the edges of sleep, he passed close and caught a glimpse of paleness and the fair fall of hair. From this he took strength.

Deor came to him. He alone for the others would not see him. A blighted sacrifice, they said . . . This at least was how Deor told it, his head drawn up and his nostrils taut in scorn.

Theuda stood before Deor. The voice was strong and as unbending as the eye below the fiery hair when Deor held forth like this. His hands were hung from his belt, his legs struck apart and there was no other possibility in his speech. Theuda was hamstrung by this fixity.

'Perhaps they will like me better when the month is gone,' laughed Theuda. And wanting still to turn him from the mood of his scorn: 'Was it to Beli you had sworn me?'

'Beli? I have heard of him. Is he not a god of sorts?'

Theuda drew back.

'A god of sorts! Is it not him that you follow then?'

Deor broke his stance and walked apart.

'Well?' said Theuda. There was still the anger of horror in him.

Deor's face was firm and set.

'You are not born of us,' he said. 'There is no talking about these things now. When the Hawthornmonth is come, you will be among us. Then we shall see.'

With this, silence stood between them for a while. Not with bitterness yet all the same cumbersome and darkening. Pride was fierce in both of them.

Later, Deor left.

It was another day soon after. Theuda came out of the hut, stepping alive and eager: there was a hunger in him. Rain had fallen but now the sky was free of blemish and crack and the sun's warmth was drawing forth thicknesses of mist from everywhere.

Theuda closed his eyes and scented the air. Wood fire and the roasting of flesh filled the west but his hunger was otherwise and he turned away east round the hill towards the woods, letting himself be drawn. In the wood, he followed the worming of a path that led down through the garlic and the dense slatwork of light among the trees. Beyond, in snatches, the plain's horizon lay under the weight of the sky. Though birds sang below him, their sounds thinned and went snuffed out at his approach so that he felt himself passing through the wood like an object of power.

The path dropped fast, falling out of the hills in tight coils. Below him, bordering the wood, ran a river, broad and calm, and beyond it lay barley and sleek green wastes starred with goats. Away to his right, a few hundred paces upriver, a large wooded island stood across the mouth of a hill stream.

Theuda braced the muscles of his thighs and shoulders and blew out a long taut breath as he peered about. Mist swathes hung low on the river, spiked through here and there by sunlight and reed. The river's flat slabs slid in under the dunes of whiteness on which pigeon-neck lights stood brought out by the sun.

He came down further, quiet and soft of foot in his intentness. He slipped out of the leaf wood and waded on through an undergrowth of briar and fern towards the water. At one moment, he stood rigid and leaned, ear-cocked and sharp, towards the island. From up there, laughter fluted high into the mist. Twice, with joy, and then silence.

He passed thigh-deep through the grass of the river bank and came to a spot where footmarks showed. There a spit of rock and shingle cut out into the water and a twist of current hung from it down the outer edge of a quiet, deep pool. Lower, just within the grasp of the mist, grew a tall spinney of reeds. Into this, Theuda withdrew, floundering in sweet mud and the succulence of growths.

Crouched in cover, he settled himself. Out in the river, fishes rose and fell with oily suck sounds. Somewhere closer, there chuckled a minute overfall. Once, far up in the hills, a shout sounded and went bounding about on itself; and another once, a river fowl kowked and passed unseen in a milling of wingstrokes. Otherwise, unchanging, there was only the cold dun bulk's secret movement and the mist packing around.

Gradually, in his staring, things of another life began to float into his mind. He poled away from them and sought to grasp at his happening self. But they persisted, coming back with all the wash of blood mess and splinterings so that little ripples started to run out on the water from his tremoring legs.

Upon the spiked gleam lay random images of his horror – of that loving, grey-haired head burst, eyes pinched in puzzlement; and of half an arm, ring-fingered, lying caught in the crook of a tree. And now, as he shook, blank-faced, the sounds came back at him too: forever the shrilling and the moans dulling and the rhythm, swish-thunk, of the great axe keeping time with his snorts of power. Smoke and heavy rain were there: and finally, among the soused ashes of his village, a sense of glory in this his first act of belief. For from that still, pearly night long before, this was what he had known was to be demanded of him. He was to put himself in her following and so was to come to know the joy of rightful service. He had seen himself dark, strangely dark and potent in this; and she, in her fairness, pale and full of light, both his and yet something cruel and unknown. He would serve her and he would have joy in her beauty: this, he had suddenly come to see, was how it had been set. Beyond was not clear but merely to follow her to be a thing of wonder that would leave fear separate and remote.

He swallowed heavily and peered out through the mist.

A tangle of voices, low and warm, passed to him upon the water. Then a quiet; but later, from nowhere, the sound of swimmers close by. Two heads broke cover upriver, sleek with water, and as the sun's fist hit them, breath and laughter sprang out of their mouths. Then, as suddenly, they had tucked under and were gone.

Theuda shifted his footing. Only the eddies of their swimming lay whorling the surface.

He shook his head. And with that, the pool's skim shattered upwards, the twin heads hooded with light and the air about breaking in bubbles and gasps.

The fair-haired girl made for the bank and rose streaming into the sun, the drops bursting sharply on her shoulders and thighs. She turned, her breasts moving like ready fruits, and with head flung towards the sky, she straddled the earth, the river water spilling off her body through the thicket of bright hair below her stomach. She was young and she was laughing.

'Dillo! Come on! Let's do it now. We can swim later.'

The other swimmer Theuda had taken for a boy. Black hair was cropped to the skull and there was sharpness in the face, much older, clean-edged and with no sign of softness. It was a boy's body too, tight-rumped, long in the leg and berry nipples on only a semblance of breasts.

For a while, the two women stood against the sun, whispering to each other with warm smiles and a secret closeness.

13

Later, when they had gone, Theuda came up from the reed bed, dead-legged and on fire.

He slipped after them through mist and sparkled bracken, pacing and holding, watchful in his pursuit, his eyes bright and hard.

He found them in a creek where a willow tree grew.

'Do it then, Dillo! You did promise!' said the blonde one.

Her words, rounded and ardent with hope, floated in the river air. Theuda blinked at her beauty.

Dillo's eyes were dark with a deepness in which the smiles struggled against the weight of knowledge.

'You did promise,' the girl said to her again. 'Dillo, I have to know! Make him come tonight. Please!'

Dillo nodded.

'Then leave me, Aithne. I'll not be long.'

Dillo, alone, smiled and made dove sounds in her throat. She walked into the river, knee-high, and stood close by the tree.

'Willow!' she called in secrecy. And again: 'Willow!'

She touched herself between her thighs and pressed her hand against the tree trunk.

'Willow of power!' she called with dove sounds.

Roots and nuts Theuda had that day. Everything had dropped from his mind but the river girl. He slept a bit at midday. There was milk in his dream and he gave it to a child to drink but the child choked and he woke with a wood pigeon close above, making its noises so that again he saw her, Aithne, the pale and fair one . . .

It was some time after this that he thought to himself: I am no longer alone.

It came out of a shimmer of his spine, a tap at his heart, an awakening. For a long time he could put no reason to it: there was only the knowledge of the skin. He moved about quietly – still feeling himself seen – just as if there were nothing in his mind. And then, in a moment, turned sharp up a bank and climbed into the young leaf of a tree. He cradled himself in the join of its limbs and let his breath slow to a nothing.

The sun passed on and the life of the wood had come well underway again when the scolding of a blackbird drew sudden alarm and then silence.

Theuda watched. And as he watched, the figure of a man, lithe, tawny of hair, came under him, walking with perfect stealth past and on into the wood.

It was thus that he came and went, both steadily and swiftly together.

Theuda frowned; for he had smelt malice on the man.

The mist had drawn back and spring burned long in the woods. But when the light began to go, the thick wreathings crept back to the lower land and came up among the trees, stifling the bright colours. The half moon rose through them and the light was flat and threatening.

Theuda perched, his face wattled with shadows, and with eyes half-shut, gave his ear to the dusk. Among the scutter of water birds and the beginnings of the night world, awareness came to him of another sound, soft, repeated, still. He heard it dreamwise, drawn on yet bound, with caught breath and his forehead crushed on the tree's bark. The calling insisted; but he stayed, his body poised with its eagerness, and the sound, sweet and determined, ruled him. In his stillness, things came to him, dark, unformed things from before and beyond so that his eyes grew wide with a violence.

When the calling broke, Theuda sprang. As if doubting, it had wavered. Then, after silence, it took up again, strong and clear. But already Theuda was loping, secret in mist and moonlight along the river bank towards the dove sounds that were spilling from low in the wood.

He stood by the willow in the creek and stared up into the trees.

The calls had changed. The dove was gone; another was there.

Theuda ran up among the trees. He reached a ridge and below him a dell was brimming with the moon.

The woman lay flat, the moss skin of a rock beneath her face. Head turned in a patch of dark, she lay and grasped at the rock with gestures of clawing. She tried dove sounds still but they were weak and broken by yelps and long breathing brought from her by the heavy-antlered buck that was working her pale bright body. Darkened spotting covered its back and the chine was streaked along with blackness, all of it flexing and straightening enormously as it drove vigorously into the woman. She called then of a sudden, with strength; and in the sound there was still the flutter of beckoning and mockery. The buck heard it and the massive frame of head and horn dropped angrily on to the slight form. Teeth worried at her open neck. She fell silent then, under the weight, and for a while the hollow had only the buck's chest noises and the flooding of the moon.

The buck's haunches began to make fiercer movements upon the woman. And then, as the head came up slow again, with antlers back, brink-taut in the pull of neck, they punched, once and twice and held. Rigid and mastering, the buck troated sullenly up into the darkness and drew off. Hunched below, the woman lay quiet, hips still drawn up against the power.

Theuda's jaws were locked round a branch. Sap tasted green and was good, all the sharpness of rancour and thwarting in it. He snarled a bit and rolled his head. Then when next he looked, the buck had gone. Standing out in the middle of the dell was Aithne.

Theuda tore himself off the tree, slavering pulp, and made bounds along the dell's rim. Noises came from close, just beyond light bushes. He sprang in mid-stride, bursting into the brake with a throttled growl and saw under the moon the buck swinging round.

He woke and still the moon hung upon the trees. Pain rose and clamped him as he moved and when he reached down, there was dampness along his flank. He lay there and felt the coldness beginning to settle into him. He looked for ways of going round the pain and at last managed, coming up slowly on the power of his arms till he was curled against a trunk.

'Now!' he called to himself as he peered uphill. 'Now!'

Half-light and the pain trapped him often as he pulled himself up the slopes. And falling brought him on to the sickle edges of new pain and pushed him towards exhaustion. Each time he huddled to rest, he stayed down longer and finally he drew himself up tight below a bank and did not move. Still he urged himself on and even saw the steps he would soon take; but the distances of time had begun to escape him. Out of his drifting mind, he spoke:

> *The ice of fear*
> *Hangs clouds about the eye.*
> *Hate has weakness for a heart.*
> *Sun-bright alone he stands*
> *Who follows fate.*

He laughed in anger at himself. Then, tapping the ground twice, he slid headlong into darkness.

Deor found Theuda in the first of birdlight. The great hound, doe-size and white, came to him and set up a calling like geese on the travel. Deor, following, patted the dog aside and bent to the fallen man.

'So what's all this then, my friend? Here, take hold of me. Can you stand?'

'Buck,' said Theuda dimly. 'Buck did it. I shall kill him.'

They made their way upwards into the bird-showered dawn.

The Hawthornmonth had come in.

They led him by torchlight in the fullness of the night. They had fired his hut first, silent and still as the timbers broke open and the sparking pillar of air spun streaming up into the void. There were six of them, one or two still youths and arrogant with their bodies and prowess. They had come unannounced to Theuda as he slept and though they were mannerly enough when they woke him, they carried knives and eyed him sideways.

When the fire had died, they lit torches from the embers and surrounded him. Ringed by flame and shadow, he was led away round the hill and up into the great woods. A number of dogs like Deor's padded on the edge of the light. They would stop, red ears pricked, and throw out honking barks at things that were not to be seen. Otherwise, only silence passed with the murmur of the pacing.

They went with a track that turned upon itself up through the trees, climbing sharply to a passageway in a bluff of flat rock. The entrance up through the cliff was narrow and there was dust and rutting in it from the passing of feet. There by the opening, motionless and axe in hand, stood Deor. His hair burst full of fire as the torch party closed with him.

'May you be welcome,' he said quietly. The eyes were still and the hand to Theuda's shoulder carried strength.

'Theuda comes to the Scaur in honour,' said Deor to the others. 'The god called him and the god held him apart. He stands pledged and free together. None may think to change this.'

They went up by the steep bend of the entrance path, Deor leading Theuda in and the lights following. At the top, they came out and a fire burned in the middle of a broad flat below cliffs that stood rising away into the night. More men were by the fire and shapes of huts lay scattered behind. Someone threw a pine branch on to the fire and it spat noise and worms of light into the hanging darkness.

By the fire, Theuda was put before a man they called Saer. He was tall, lime-washed of hair and dark-skinned. He said little but the movement of flamelight put images of peace and quiet laughter on him so that Theuda could only look at him and be silent with awe.

And, of a sudden, the whole of it was as a thing remembered. Come and gone as a flying spark, it and the dream were happening together and Theuda's heart rose out of him.

'Saer is the Tineman,' said Deor.

And Theuda, still carried on the surge, fell to his knees.

'No,' said Saer and touched him on the head. 'Come.'

But Theuda was speaking:

He has travelled far
Who reaches home.
Warm is the fire,
Strong the blood
Of friends in meeting.

A soft undertow of voices moved in the night. Saer spoke across it:

'It is as Deor said. The way of words is surely yours. A wordspeaker stands by himself: it is for him to show what is.'

'I know nothing of this,' replied Theuda. 'The words make themselves. I am no part of them.'

Around him, they still mouthed wonder and there was a steady restlessness in their feet as they looked at him.

Across the flames, a man was standing. Theuda saw him and swallowed his shout:

'Buck!'

Their eyes struck flint-hard. Sinews were taut.

Deor took Theuda's elbow and drew him gently out of the grip of his anger.

'The Men of Scaur do not fight their fights here. To fight here brings only weakness.'

Theuda heard this and then he had a smile on his face.

'I do not need to fight him. He is nothing to me.'

The men made a ring round the fire. There were fourteen of them and Theuda watched as Saer held high a forked stick. When the stick fell from the edge of night into the flames, a great shout went up. Later, Deor told him that it was the god entering the hidden heart.

Theuda now was there. Yet still he was apart. It was not said but it was so. Day followed on day and there was warmth towards him; but his hut was on the edge and faced away and at special moments distance was expected of him. There was soreness in this for him: but he stared at his belief and was strong.

19

'And the women?'

Beohrt the fleshman looked at him out of the shagginess of hair and beard.

'The women?'

'Yes. Where are they?'

'Why, down there! Where else?' he answered with a sweep of the arm towards the river.

'Do they not come to the Scaur?'

'To the Scaur? No, that has never happened. It would be a thing badly done. Nobody has entrance here. There is the Tineman and his tanist and us twelve. That is all. And now, it is true, there is you who came with the god.'

'You have a woman down there?'

Beohrt brayed out a laugh.

'I have women and other women. I do not want.'

'You don't have one woman then? One out of all the others?'

Beohrt's laugh died.

'That would be an ugly thing. Nobody would do it.'

He blew his nose into the undergrowth in disgust.

With Beohrt were the other fleshmen, Fer and Romac, men hard of lung and leg. It was for them to assure flesh for the Scaur. The others went often to the hunt as well and so honoured the god; but of what they took, much went down to the riverland for the women. From them in return, the Men of Scaur had bread and milk and cheese.

Theuda went out to the forest with Kuno, one of the youths. They went far that day for now the sun was burning higher and there was all the life of spring in their limbs. They struck across slopes and streams, beds of fern and hidden clearings where warmth lay penned; and passed roving on into the trees over moss and piled rockfall. As they moved and waited, each turn of head cuffed them with blows of light.

A stream fell steeply and the sun was in the water. Sheltered in the brightness and tumbling noise stood a young buck. Theuda, coming ahead of Kuno, paused unseen. He drew back his spear and his eye held the deer's chest. And then he was throwing, his arm pulling hard with all the force of shoulder over braced legs. But with this, a flurry form was beside him at speed; and as the spear went, he was knocked, out and sideways, heavily into the grass. The deer kicked up and was gone.

'Are you mad?' Kuno's voice bit.

Theuda sprang up and was full of fight.

'What was that for?'

'Would you shame yourself? It is forbidden you. It is to anyone coming new to the Scaur till they have been to the feast.'

'I know nothing of any feast,' answered Theuda shortly.

'The feast at Ura,' said Kuno. 'Till then you may hunt otherwise but you shall not take of the god himself.'

'Which god is that then?' He was still at variance.

'But, Theuda, the Horn Fellow! It is he we follow. It is what we are. Buck and doe – they are all part of him who feeds us.'

Theuda stayed broken off in thought. Then:

'And Saer?'

'Saer is the Horn Fellow's Tineman. He grows with the sun and must fall to his rival, the Tineman who will rule with the other sun, the sun on the wane. It is how it has always been.'

'His rival?'

'Just so. The rival who loves him, who is his other self. The Tineman's tanist.'

'And the tanist? Saer's tanist?'

'It is Deor.'

Theuda met his dream again. There, as before, waited the darkness and its happiness. And towards it went pacing the great buck on fire, led by the woman with her fairness of hair and her hidden face. And in his dream Theuda was with them, they who followed the buck. So now, quite newly, he saw that to be of the Men of Scaur, that alone could be his course, that alone gave entrance to what had been called of him.

'And the Men of Scaur themselves? How do they come to be?'

'The new Tineman takes his tanist from them. Then it is

21

that one more must come from the river. He is chosen from among those born of the god.'

They sat long there. The sun grew; the water went unchanged. Theuda learned.

He looked again at Kuno. Deor's brow was there and set of jaw; and the eyes too. They were green and bright and with the sharpness of them there was nothing that could be missed. There was beauty in him, in features and all the evenness of moving. With a bow, he was beyond touching. Even among the skills of the Men of Scaur, he was spoken of as Kuno the archer.

'But is Deor your father then?'

'My father? How do you mean? My mother was Luned. The god made me with her at the day of Ura. The Ten were there. That is how it always is.'

'The Ten? Kuno, again I must ask.'

Kuno gave a small laugh and touched him on the cheek.

'Yes, it is true, you have much still to know. The Ten – they are those who go to the mountain with the Tineman at Ura.'

'You must tell me these things, Kuno. My learning is from you.'

Later they killed a boar, Theuda holding back Kuno's arrows so that he could take it on the spear. There was blood and noise and all the joy of a proper death. Kuno did the rites.

Theuda watched Buck with care. Still the rancour lay within but now sense was ruling him for he did not care to spoil his standing in the Scaur. He learned that Buck called himself Cynric and had for a friend one named Corm. There was closeness among all the Men of Scaur but towards Cynric and Corm, the others' love was guarded. Theuda saw this.

In those days of steady suns and strength and by their nights of stars, Theuda's mind came often to Aithne the river girl. Now she was of his dream: he saw her, the fair one who would lead, whom he would rule and serve. He had grown to a sureness of it. But he knew too that Cynric's death alone could cleanse her for him. Between this and his good sense, he felt himself pinned.

And as Theuda watched Cynric so too did Deor watch Theuda: with care. Only once did Deor speak of it.

'Saer has me say that his day lies close. And that it brings dismay if any of the Men of Scaur should suffer ill in this season.'

'I have no mind for such things, Deor. I have thoughts elsewhere.' He made a pause and then: 'Deor, I have never spoken to you of my coming here.'

'Men say what they want to say, Theuda,' replied Deor. 'It is for you to speak of such things. We hold you as you are, not as you were.'

Theuda nodded slowly.

'Before,' he said, 'my life was quite otherwise. It was last summer that the bidding suddenly came. And it stayed, both in my waking and my sleep, till finally I no longer had the choice of things. I knew then what had to be done. And so . . . and so I put away that life and left. As if lost yet somehow sure, I found my way here. And now – now I can but follow where I am taken. I have great strength of trust in what one day must be mine.'

He turned away from Deor. The utterness of his truth was upon him.

'My life's end I am to find in joy,' he said. 'This I know. And it is to be in service to the Men of Scaur. There is to be some way of which as yet I cannot tell.'

Deor too was carried by Theuda's speaking of his truth. He clasped him and said with warmth:

'Theuda, this is the breathing of the god. For each man, there can be only the knowing of his purpose. When this happens then truly gladness holds us all for him.'

The darkened forest and the paling sky alone were there.

Then, after a silence of depth, Deor spoke again:

'Men meet then go on their ways. Others may stay and the years themselves put a binding upon them. But, Theuda, there are men who meet and though they should part at the next sunfall, their meeting has been a branding. Is this not so?'

Theuda turned to Deor.

'Yes,' he said.

There was the desolation of joy in his voice; and, around it, an immense stillness, tender and with the might of iron.

23

3

Now no longer the days but their hours lay on him. The dream and its woman had him with such seeming anger of purpose that other things, the hunt and the comradeship of the Scaur, were all but by the by. His head echoed with Aithne. In the Scaur, he saw only Cynric.

He saw how Cynric spoke little and was like a cat in his stealth. He looked at the skin, child-smooth and dull with the sun, and the beauty of it was horror to him. Yet it was in the eyes that there showed what lay veiled in the body. They were cowled and still and in his silences they spoke. Theuda had met the milling strength of a bare-fighter; but against the shadowed light of Cynric's eye, he had nothing.

'Buck!' He shot the word up into the darkness and bit it off with gritted jaw.

And: 'Buck!' again, under the vaulting of the pines at the height of day. 'It shall be! I say it!'

He ringed Cynric with his awareness and Cynric felt it and moved in loops about him. Words they never had: there were none for it.

The shadow nests plumped up and were heavy with the settlement of birds as evening grew. Breathlessness held firm among the trees. The young stars stood about a slip of moon and all the imprint of past heat hung scent and memory within the forest. Sounds – crack and snort – were vast and unowned so that distances opened and closed in the crazing of half-light.

He might have gone before yet had watched the sun all the way down the sky before he moved. He knew his need for the hour of change. Now he struck down the slopes with a tautness and speed that were a release from the wait.

Under glow and glimmer, he stood at the stream mouth and stared across at the island in the river. Lights flared and away among the trees at the island's prow, a core of fire lay lodged in the undergrowth of night. Bursts of voices flowered into the sky. Then only stream and river ran as one.

Lost in dreaming, he waded slowly into the water. Firmly his treading took him to mid-stream. Coolness purled about his chest; a sleek current ate softly at his balls. In his pausing, an owl called from the land and he saw himself a dwarf growth in the flood.

Up against the island, the waters hung torpid beneath bushes. Theuda seized roots and drew himself, in serpent form, towards the fire and sound. No plan took him; his need and belief were all. Still now, among the small dark turmoils of his going, he saw completeness closing with him, felt his prey of happiness warm beneath him and pressed forward, inflexible and full of cold laughter.

'Hoiha!' A bark from the bushes and the soaring shrill of a whistle.

Theuda hung. Feet came fast with a gathering crowd of flames, back from the bank yet close. Women, young and old, peered down at him. Here and there among them, bellies rounded with child were bare and had rings of dark expanding on them. Some mouths smiled but the eyes were harsh and set.

'Aithne!' called Theuda. 'Where is Aithne?' Nobody moved. 'I have to speak with her!'

He tried to pierce the flarelight. Only eye and arm and dazzle looked back at him. But a stirring was happening on the edge of the light. He turned to it and a heavy mesh struck and folded over him. A howl of gloating tore open the crowd. Light and limb poured forward on to the bank and the caterwaul of triumph broke over Theuda while the tugging drew about him. He plunged away, groping back for the knife.

Rope squeezed at his feet. And with his stumbling, it sprang under his heels and went tight. The lights wheeled and water took him, angrily, so fast that he had drawn only half his breath. He twisted up for more, took it beneath the thunderous faces of the women and again was gone. His hand, through the net, had the knife and waited for them to haul him in. Dimly still he could hear the racketing behind the enormousness within his head. As he hung rump-high, it burst into him that they had no thought to bring him in, that this was the end they had in mind for him, with slowness and shame.

Fear fury took hold. But with it came a body knocking against him and a hand, as cool and light as a fish, that ran lithe between his legs and seized him. The grip changed from tight to fierce. Theuda roared in his lungs and swung with the knife. The hand went.

Now he sawed at the drawstring, violent with the life urge, sawed and ripped in foam till of a sudden the net gave and, like fluxed bowels, he was spilled out into the quiet drift of the river.

He broke surface and ate at the air with gollops and madness. The flares moved on the island, keeping pace, and the cries were of abuse that came powerlessly with rocks and stones. He sank away again, leaving his face alone above, and let the river have him. He was doubled with pain, knees drawn in and his face twisting; but it was the stunning of shock that left him so disarmed.

Stars were above and all the colour forms of evening's falling. He saw the herons cross, the wing of duck and the scurry flight of flittermice. Silver flesh grazed against his back; and a water hen, met unawares, oared and strode herself away into a quarter of early night.

He blinked and sank and rose again, ponderous with the water's rhythm, and let his eyes close to lose all. On, logwise and dozing, he went, buoyed and weighted; and the violence seeped from him. Then, at last, far out, his anger slept. He rolled and swam.

In a small backwater he lay grounded. He groaned aloud at his pain and crawled to the bank. A willow tree grew there and a woman's voice said:

'Come, you are tired.'

He swung fist and arm blindly and a body gave before them. He crouched at the wait. A shape moved on the grass and spoke quietly.

'Put away your fear,' it said. 'I am not one of them. I am Dillo.'

'Dillo?'

'Yes.'

'I am Theuda.'

'I know.'

She led him. And he went with her for her voice was such.

'Are you hurt?' she asked, seeing his hand at his groin.

'They would have torn them from me, I think.'

'Yes,' she replied, 'they would. I have something for it though.'

Now darkness rose beneath and steadily rose again in force. The embering light shrank away still higher. Then, in a pace, it was quite gone. Shapes stood everywhere about, undisclosed. Even smells lay crushed now, the ooze chill covering all. Theuda kept close and copied Dillo's legs. Tiredness stalked through his body and sent him tripping. Then at last, there where the bank rose high, he smelt wood-smoke. He looked about: but tree and river alone were there.

He shook his head.

'Dillo!' he called at the emptiness. 'Dillo!'

A hand touched him on the ankle and the earth spoke.

'Here! Down here!'

With his mind struggling against it, the hand led him down a hole. It dropped shaftlike and opened round a bend into a lair. There a small fire burned and threw its light into Dillo's face. Fern bed and skins lay against a wall, with water and a bowl. The edgeless waver of the flamelight covered all.

He lay on the ferns and watched the fire smoke drawing off into a vent. The net strands were weaving about him still and the howl and that fineness of hand reaching in to take him. But he rolled his head and she was there at the fire. Water steamed with the smoke.

He drank her drink, slowly and without care. It was sour and rich together and had the taste of deep undergrowth in it. With crossed legs, she sat apart and the silence of the night lay easily between them. Her eyes though were on him and he knew them so, dark and huge and horizonless. It was beyond him to turn to her.

Nothing moved.

Later, he began to speak. The words rose up in his mouth in a moment when he thought himself asleep. As out of the opening of a fist, tight and hard, things of beyond came; and quested things too, all of them held and released without pain. So that then he laughed with it, laughed at this sudden strange closeness to what was sheer and clear-bright within.

Gradually the dance of the fire slowed. Theuda went with it, his body falling to rest; and so the lair settled under the dull mash of light. Yet there was no sleep in it. Now the stillness brought before him vastness and remote power so that, with it, he could only let the mere shape of words slide from his lips. He stood alone, no sureness beneath and tower-high walls of dark shining about him. And in his each breathing of words, there was completeness.

Later, at the fire's death, his pain came to him again and he spoke a name. His belt loosened and his legs parted so that he felt himself astraddle assuaging cool then cold then warm till at last light and pain went out together and, close by his ear, came an echoed sound, soft like the breeze:

'Sleep!'

When the sun broke soaring above the hill and the martins of the bank were aloft, Dillo beckoned Theuda back from the river. On a small flat of grass and bareness, an oak tree grew alone. High in a bowl of its branches they sat faced together and feathers of warm wind moved about them. She offered him leaf and they both took it and so sharpness came and understanding. Her hands, long-fingered, rested and her eyes looked beyond the hills as she waited for him.

'Dillo of the Bank,' he began, 'tell me of Aithne.'

'You must first know of the holm,' she replied.

'You have been there then?'

'I was young then,' she replied. 'They told me later how they had found me on the banks and taken me with them to the holm. Ten winters I was there with them. I learned to follow their ways and to know the truths of Alphito to whom they are sworn. But always I was trouble to them, they said.'

'Trouble? But how?'

'They said that their laws were as nothing to me. Perhaps this was so – but, in truth, it was other things. They told me that secrets shared made strength, that secrets held to a person alone were wrong and harmful. They said I had secrets.'

'It was true?'

She nodded.

'And so it must always be. They are part of me.'

For a long while they listened to the earth giving out its noises.

'So they put you out then?'

Dillo's eyes smiled but her broad mouth was firm.

'Just so. Now they let me be though still they come with the moon to shave me. They think the cutting will stop my powers.' She laughed. 'I let them think it.'

'And the women of the holm? What had I done to be set upon so?'

'Theuda, you must know that the holm is Alphito's. No man may go to it. Your rashness took you there. They would have cut your man's parts from you before they landed you.'

Theuda bit at his lip.

'And then?'

'I saw it happen once,' she said slowly. 'When I was small. It is no way to die.'

Theuda looked away.

'And Alphito? As one to follow, what is she?'

'Ah, Alphito!' And smiling blankness rolled briefly over Dillo's eyes. 'Cool and white and the bringer of wonder and fear she is. She is the moon and the pearl of barley and the great pale sow. She is the terrible whiteness that is both glory of beauty and also disfiguring destruction. She rules the hidden strengths, the ways of innerness and is in the winds of the night. The women know her by nature: they are of her and can never be completely otherwise.'

'So you too follow her then?'

'Of course – and with joy. But not only her. I am part of all things.'

For a while, Theuda's thoughts lay heavily on him. Flung far above, a falcon was calling.

'But how?' he broke out suddenly, with fist striking knee. 'How shall I come to her?'

Dillo swung her head slowly.

'This I cannot say for you, Theuda. In these days of the Hawthorn she stands apart. She wears the band. She goes to the mountain at Ura.'

'So she is chosen?'

'Yes, she is chosen. From now, it will be as always.' And so Dillo told further of the ways of the holm. How, at this season, ten of the untouched women of age were marked out. Once they had taken of the Tineman at Ura, each must lie with the next man she saw. And for this reason, they were kept sightless until they had come to the mountain on the following day. 'I tell you this that you may better understand. No woman of the holm will speak to you of such things.'

Again Theuda was pinned under by thought. His head weighted him forward; his eyes stood lost in the scoring of the bark. Bent over himself, he was following what was to be as into a mist. Then at last he straightened himself and brought his face before Dillo's. For a while they sat so, high and under the sun, firm of spine and motionless together. And he felt all the strength of her eyes: for her seeing passed into him as light into water.

'And you, Dillo – will you help me? She would come for you.'

Dillo opened into a smile.

'It is true. For me, they all come. It is what I have. And most hate me for it.' She let a pause come in and her eyes rested on him sideways. Then: 'Yes, I shall help you, Theuda.'

They took more leaf and, there together, gradually heard everything. The sun had already passed beyond when they came down from the oak.

There was height in the rock and he watched her from afar. She came alone, head down, along the river, and she walked as if set about by dreams. The green she wore was part of the woods; only the scarlet that banded her head of fair hair marked her. Even from the distance of his stand, he saw the way she used her body and his bowels clenched. A while longer he stayed on the watch and then he sprang down. Joy of hope made him leap harelike on the hillside as he made for the meeting stone.

Breezes pawed the late sunshine. Mast was underfoot and all the secrecy of spirit places was about, the beeches vast with their flying archways and branch-ends sprung low by the ground leaving only a soft fire of light on the forest floor. The great stone lay tilted in moss. A ring of signs lay cut upon it among the lichen scabs. Fear and safety filled the place.

Her humming came slowly by the path. But reaching the bank top and seeing him, she swallowed her music and drew herself in behind a tree. Elderberry's darkness was stained in on her brow and lips and gave shadow to her beauty. Her eyes, just seen, were grey and large with mistrust. They watched and waited and he would have spoken but did not know how. Then, trying her, he stood forward; but with squirrel speed she had gone. Later, when he had lain back, seemingly at rest, she was there again. In stillness, as if from sleeping, he spoke her name. Silent and root-bound she stayed. But again he called. And then again and now with words and throat sounds to fend her fear away. And slowly, by this edging on, she came at last to stand before him, hard by the great stone.

'You know me then?' he asked.

Gulping, she gave him a sharp nod.

31

'Yet still I bring terror to you. Why?'

Quickly her eyes went left and right and then centred back on him. Her lips made shapes but stopped.

He breathed: 'Aithne!' And then said more clearly: 'You have the beauty that men speak of. I did not know it could be.'

'Who are you?' Her voice crept through the stillness. 'Why did you call me here?'

And now Theuda spoke strongly:

'That you may know. You are to be mine: I am to serve you. And this I now claim of you for it is set.'

She stepped back. Disgust snarled in her face.

'You are mad!' Of a sudden, she had come beyond her fear. 'Can you not see? I wear the band. I am chosen. Have you no shame to speak so to me? And in the Hawthornmonth at that!'

'The Hawthornmonth?'

'Yes. No person couples in these days. We wait and we prepare. This is known by all.'

Theuda blinked.

'Then,' he replied, 'I shall make no further mention of it now. Yet still I say that I shall serve you, that I shall protect and make gain for you.'

'For me? Me alone?' Her voice had come childlike out of the hush.

Theuda's eyes dropped from her delight. There was a leaping within him.

> *The wind stands high;*
> *The sun burns over*
> *All the hills.*
> *Close lies the edge:*
> *For ever the fall.*
> *Talons hook*
> *The heart of joy.*

His voice had sounded from far down with all the heaviness of wonder. And now he stood there confounded by the speaking; while the girl had fallen to a crouch upon the leaves.

'You spoke words,' she said.

Theuda looked at her. He was still dumb with his confusion.

'Yes, you did,' she said, 'you spoke words!' She was finding herself again. 'Then you must know things, things that others cannot know.'

And carefully her hand came and touched him.

'Your arm,' said Theuda, 'how did that happen?' Mottled red, a cloth was bound about her forearm.

Still hunkered down, she fell quiet again. Yet her eyes held his with fierceness.

'How?' he demanded and harsh tones were rising in his voice.

But she would not speak. Her teeth were buried in the bed of her lip.

'It was you!' he burst out. 'The other day, in the water. It was you! I cut you.'

His hand was already on his knife and his spirit choked on the sadness of his anger. He turned aside to rid himself of her.

'You called me. By name,' he heard her say gently behind him. 'There was no choice for me. It is the law.'

He nodded his forehead fury hard against a tree. When he turned round, she was gone.

In the Scaur, it was all otherwise.

Now by stages, with the growth of days, Saer was drawing himself in. The others felt the windless calm about him and lived with restraint and the gravity of awe. Deor was much with Saer at this time, keeping distance yet always there at hand. Without him, Theuda went often to the hunt with Kuno and both found strength and closeness in the sharing of triumphs.

Two of the men, Leudi and Ansi, the tall, smooth-pated ones by whom Theuda had been taken to serve as the Sorel, were largely apart too for they were the Tineman's men. Then there were the three fleshmen; and also Cynric with his friend Corm. Otherwise there was Uhtred the runner, Brun who knew of stars and the curing of dogs, Eudo the smith and young Witu, bright of mind and a climber of rocks.

There was a day when the sun stood fixed in the sky. Heat lay in siege on the forest hills and up at the Scaur it was ranked massively at the edge of the shade.

'It is not the same any more.'

One of the bodies, flat beneath the pines, had spoken.

'What?' answered Uhtred from his dozing.

'The choosing of them,' said Beohrt. 'Before, when we used to fight for it, the place in the Scaur was well earned. Now, without the fight and with the women having a say in the choice, it is not the same.'

'So?' Another voice. It was Brun's.

'So they could make use of it. Listen – if they can say which of the men is to come here, in time they might use it to try and control us.'

'Control us! But why? You must have taken the sun, Beohrt!'

Laughter came and went. When the mockery gave out, a bee's flight was in the silence.

But later Romac spoke:

'I think Beohrt is right. I have heard things.'

'What things?'

'Things. About the holm. There is bad feeling there. Anger. I think they are planning.'

'Planning what?' There was a flaring-up in Uhtred's voice.

'Things. I think Beohrt is right.'

In these times, Theuda saw how it was with Saer the Tineman and watched him letting the days of his fate put their shape on him. And now Theuda asked many things of Kuno and Kuno spoke to him, giving clearer form to what they of the Scaur held to in mind and trust.

Good fortune – Kuno told him – they strove to win by giving honour to the god in the chase. Whatever they might pursue, the hunt was never to be undertaken lightly for it was always entered into in his name. To the Men of Scaur, he was the keeper of all things of the earth.

'But what then of Ura when the god joins with Alphito, the white one?' asked Theuda. 'As keeper of all things of the earth, does he have need of her?'

'Need? There is no needing in the god. He is all.'

'Then why?'

'It is more a giving,' replied Kuno, eyeing him. 'He puts his power into her that new life should be born for the Scaur.'

A frown held Theuda silent a while.

'And the children born of the god? What becomes of them?'

'For seven winters the boys stay on the holm. Then the women take them upriver to the place where there live the other sons of the god. There they learn strength and skill in preparation for the day when they may be chosen for the Scaur.'

'And the girls?'

'The girls are put away at birth. It must be so.'

These things Theuda learned.

And then, under awnings of heat and harsh skies, the Oak-month was upon them. Weapons of the forest were put aside: Ura stood but eleven days off.

It was during this lulling before the feast that Theuda was once more beset by thoughts of Aithne. For the Scaur's peace, he had sought to drive himself from his dream of her; but this was not to be and the stern goad of memory came in at him so that he sprang up in the night pricked by horror of his loss. Below a glimmering of moon he paced and the rocks were silent about him.

Birdlight found him in the forest, passing down among the clamour and the wards of heavy green. Fervour had him fast and he moved knowing the shortness of his time. Simple longings were with him too: for her and for the riverland with its water-runs where fronds hung flagging slowly in the streams. But before and beyond these longings was need: that the days of Ura should lead him in. And the river girl – she was to be for him the gateway.

The sun's bow braced across the sky. Theuda watched and

saw no sign. But when he came to the stone, she was there, faced towards him and waiting.

'You did not come,' she said. 'You spoke words to me and then did not come again. I have waited often.'

'I did not know,' he answered. 'Not till now.'

They walked far and swam where rocks slabbed into slow depths. In their swimming, he touched her and she said: 'No.' Later, at the very height of the day, they took themselves to a covert. From there, they looked to the flatlands beyond. Great heat lay there at work.

She was looking down, seeing herself.

'When I think of you and me,' she said, 'the feeling is so strong that it puts fear in me. It must be a sickness that I have. One day, just like that, I saw you and fell ill with it. I do not understand what you have done to me. And I am sure they will send me away for it.' She laughed a little wildly; then tears came.

'But it is good – not sickness. It makes strength.'

'But how am I to speak to them of it? How? They will not understand either. Such a thing can never have been before.'

Theuda laughed and whispered to her:

'Then do not speak of it. It is for you: it is for me.'

'A secret, you mean?' She looked up through the tears. 'But that would be terrible. It would be even worse.'

Now Theuda came each day to the riverland and a bond of power grew about them. By night, his dreaming fell away into peace. He lived bright with belief and its joys.

Aithne sat apart from Theuda. She wore the band and so it was right. Yet now it had grown irksome to them both and with each gnawing circle of the sun, there was forever a worsening. But then came a day when Theuda spoke to Aithne with breathlessness.

'They are chosen!' he burst out, his body still plucked by the pulses of his running. 'They took twigs. I saw them. They are the Ten. It is they who go to the mountain. And Buck! He is one of them!'

'Buck?'

'Yes, Buck. Cynric. The one who . . .'

'Who what?'

'Who . . . wore the skin! That night in the dell.'

A new smile of interest crept into Aithne's eyes. They looked round a corner at him.

'He is not a friend then?'

'A friend! I shall kill him! I swear it!'

Aithne walked to a tree and her hand stroked at the roughness of bark.

'I shall!' growled Theuda. 'I swear so!'

She nodded and was smiling to the tree. Speaking to it also:

'Could you be one of the Ten, Theuda?'

'How? I am scarcely one of the Men of Scaur.'

She was thinking.

'But when one goes, one comes in. Is that not so?'

And she was away, light of foot among the trees, so that he was having to spring fast to catch her.

'You are touching me, Theuda.' Her smile looked down at his grip of her arm. But with his freeing of her, again she made as if to leave.

'Aithne!' he called. 'Wait!'

And she stopped for him.

'But there is no killing a man in the Scaur these days before Ura.'

'Things can be otherwise than what is seen,' she said.

The next day she gave him a twist of leaves.

'A salve,' she said with wryness. 'One touch to the blood and a beast of the forest would be eating earth before dayfall.'

'Even the larger beasts?'

'No,' she replied. 'For them perhaps longer.'

Theuda climbed back towards the Scaur. He was slow and full of weight. And he was casting about, searching. He bit his teeth together and spoke keenly inside himself:

'To the god I swear myself! Now let him be of guidance to me!' And in speaking so, he stopped.

Away and over the valley, a crowned buck was watching him. It stood and was as if of stone. Theuda stared back at it.

And later, he was still staring. As the sun moved on above, the steadiness between them grew tauter till finally all else came to fall away. Theuda was braced; for a great burning was passing through him. He made to cry out his fear but his lips opened on an empty throat. He blew noises from his nose and his chin struck forward. But at last he could hold no longer. He bleated as he fell; then roared bullwise into the deep earth.

Later, he went quietly on up to the Scaur. Now belief was again with him and all of a grim joy.

At the Scaur, he found Leudi and Ansi by the huts. They were busy unwrapping a great skin with its antlered head; and the colouring of it, verging on the very pitch of night, brought him sudden recall.

'It is the Tineman's,' said Leudi.

'He alone may wear it,' said Ansi. 'Its darkness is power.'

And Theuda left them and stood apart to give his thanks to the god.

'Now it will be easy,' he said. And with that, he went to the forest again and found himself a bramble shoot.

It was soon after, when some of them were plucking fruits, that once more chance was given to Theuda by the god.

Close by, Cynric stood planted in the growth underfoot and was reaching far past a prickly bush for the fruit. Theuda smiled; then turned aside and, making tight the coil of bramble on his finger, he dipped the thorn.

'Pass them back to me, the fruits,' he said, laughing, full of light.

'Ah, so now you choose to speak to me,' said Cynric, half-smiling and sneered-up in his reply.

'The god has his times,' said Theuda. Joy was holding him.

'It is so,' said Cynric and reached high past the bush.

Theuda's thorn tore Cynric lightly on the neck. Then the bramble shoot had gone.

'Buck!' he breathed.

4

Dark swelterings hung in the dregs of daylight. All through the day, a thickening had grown: breezes dropping back and a cast-colouring of bronzeness seeping in overhead. Now the far edgelands muttered sullenly and flocks of brilliance hawked among the hills. Below the Scaur, the forest waited, silent and hostile.

The ale was passed. Wrought by the weight of heat, they sat by the flare and laughed deep in the bowls. The pale drink, crushed out of the heather, brought strength and spirit back to them: yet still the anger of storm hung over and they were wary.

After the picking of the fruit, Theuda had come up with Corm near the huts. There was meanness around the flesh of Corm's mouth. Pitch hair and eyes winter-blue gave to him the weakness of beauty.

'Tell Cynric,' Theuda had said with hushed violence, 'tell him that tonight I shall speak of him. He would do well to be ready.'

'And why should he care? What could you have to say of him? You are not even one of us.'

'Hear me, Corm! It is the time for things to be known. Cynric is one of the Ten. Now go!'

And so, in the ale ring, Theuda sat watched and waiting. Corm was there, without speech and anger-eager with the bowl: soon his eyes were hard and bright. Elsewhere storm sounds were growing and the earth was covered with the bursting of lights.

Cynric came. He put aside his bowl and sat himself close to Theuda.

'You threaten me,' he said with darkness and his eyes were pouchy and his forehead sown with sweat.

'There is a truth to be told.'

'A truth? What truth?'

'The skin, the great skin. You wore it. I saw you and you know it.'

'You would say that? Here, in the Scaur? They would laugh, I tell you. And then they would put you out.'

'Perhaps. Yet still it must be.'

Then of a sudden Cynric's mouth was by Theuda's ear. He heard the drag drawing of breath and words that were spat.

'Then do so, you tyke! But I tell you – you will go for it. And they will say too that it is rightful that I should take you in blood. And so I shall! And gladly!'

Storm light threw up into Cynric's face. Spittle stood froth white at his mouth; lines of sneering pulled up at his nostrils and there was twisting. The eyes burned dark in the hoods.

In the sky, the drumwork had moved in and clattering and crack noises were in it as it held overhead. And with its close bursting, Theuda went too. For a moment the river girl was before him; then there was left for him only Cynric and loathing.

'Buck!'

Theuda's bowl shattered against the hut.

'I call witnesses!' he shouted and the sky broke over him. 'I tell you this – a man has worn the Tineman's skin.'

Some sprang; others cried out in anger. Kuno was at Theuda's side.

'Theuda, have care! This is a thing of horror you say! Let me tell them it was the ale speaking.'

But Theuda was beyond, his jaw shivering with a fury.

'A man has worn the skin,' he repeated. 'This I say. It is what is true.'

'Saer should be called and Deor too,' said Romac and others shouted up with him.

Then Corm spoke, with eyes lit and sharp of tongue.

'Who is this man that he thinks to say such things? He is not one of us.'

'He came to us in honour,' said Uhtred. 'Remember – it is as Deor said.'

'Then he shall make proof of his words!' cut back Corm.

The splitting above that came after drove all back. It burst on them, with tearing and whiplash, and broke out into blows and bounding of hollowness. Behind it, drawn in, came a coil of wind and then the first of rain, fat and heavy as oil.

In the hut, they were waiting for Saer and Deor. Theuda was on his own, watching the silence clasping the Men of Scaur. Rain thundered. He took more ale and drank swiftly: now sureness was warm within him. Cynric stood across with Corm and his eyes had a grip on Theuda.

Kuno came with the Tineman and his tanist. Saer stood and his sight was on the depths of himself; Deor it was who spoke to Theuda.

'You must give a name,' he said calmly. 'It is a thing said and so there is need for saying more.'

'It was Cynric,' answered Theuda. 'It was he who wore the skin. I saw him. It was at the end of the Willowmonth.'

No movement came from Deor but his eyes passed over Theuda's face. Theuda met them.

'It is not your anger speaking?' asked Deor quietly.

'No. I tell you: I saw him in the skin. It must be said.'

'And for proof, Theuda? They will ask for proof.'

So Theuda gave his nod and Deor turned about. He called across the storm:

'Cynric, you are named! It is said you wore the skin. Will you give us answer to this?'

'It is ill said, a lie!' Cynric's flat words were spoken against his teeth.

'There is no lie but yours!' Theuda threw back. 'You wore it! That night of the Willowmonth. You were with the woman. In the dell by the river.'

'I know a dell there, it is true. And perhaps it could be that I have been there by night. But the skin – never! That would be madness!' And he let a smile open and fade for Theuda.

41

From out of the peening of the rain, the Tineman spoke hugely:

'An end to this! Let the accuser bring proof. This is how it is and has always been.'

The Tineman's words left them rocklike. Theuda had all eyes.

He stood there, feeling the ale's work lying loosely in him and the greatness of a sealed anger doubling itself towards power and an effortless scorn. Again his bowl brimmed and was drained and then, with face closed off, he rolled his head and spoke:

> *Words die hard:*
> *Men with ease.*
> *Blackness rots*
> *The flesh of lies.*
> *The rising sun*
> *Will brighten into*
> *Joy of truth.*

A juddering murmur troubled among the men. Theuda stepped to Saer and with solemnness asked him the grace of a night.

The day went out into night with unbroken storm.

Sun struck high and clear and soon drew off the sappiness of earth as morning grew. The Men of Scaur came together from the huts till only Corm and Cynric were lacking from the ring. Deor went to them and called them out before the Tineman.

Jubilating birds rose in the sky on the shift of winds as the two men came to join the others. Faces turned aghast to watch. For Cynric was purpling and bladdered up about the neck; and so weakened that Corm had him dragging in the dirt. His eyes popped and the larded jowls were worked with patches of darkening. Drivelling hung from drumskin lips.

The Tineman's voice burst the circle's rim and threw up a fan of pigeons from the trees.

'Shame, Cynric, shame! Pride of power has done this. It

blackens in you now. Will you cry denial still?'

Cynric gawked. A pinched eye darted at Theuda.

'Answer me!'

Saer's shout jolted the air. Cynric staggered and a bubble of a word blew from his lips. Saer had tears at his eyes: for a moment sadness of hope had risen through anger. He shook his head once, twice, slowly; then raised the crossed fingers.

Corm fell back. Leudi came with Ansi and were quick. Still the birds sang high as the tall men worked the bowstring on Cynric. Snottering and a mess of sounds came. It was truly a shameful death.

For a day, Theuda ran free from his course. The dog he now had was with him and together they went out to the hills of the forest. Tracks they climbed that led them high, there on wooded ridges close below the sun, lung-tight with speed and all the fiery sharpness of the air; and thence on down the slopes of shadows, hung with waters storming their way among the eyrie cliffs.

It was a cleansing: fear went and again he stood close to his belief.

Deor met him by the Scaur. Brotherhood was strong.

'Saer sends me. The place stands free for you and Ura is close. Will you be of us and come as one of the Ten to the feast?'

Theuda patted the dog and looked up. Gladness was creased on his face.

'With all my heart,' he said.

It was by a wild dusklight that he saw her once more before the feast. There was yawing and rushing in the massive rollers of green and the madness of wind was tearing limbs in the wood under a havoc of noise. They had to shout their words.

Her speaking had cramps in it.

'I am frightened,' she said.

And then, under cover of the storm, she told him of one of

the women of the holm, one named Ead, as tall and as strong as a man, who had long wanted harm for her. Some years before, the white one had touched Ead's face; and since then, she had been driven only by dreams of power and vengeance.

'I mocked her once,' said Aithne in her misery. 'I was younger then and she had frightened me. It was in my fear that I spoke cruelly of her face. She has never forgiven me for it.

'And now Ead says that her girl, her friend, has seen us often together. As I wear the band, she seeks to make something of this. Theuda, I must go! If I am found with you now, they will kill me for it.'

And it was then, as she was trying to leave, that Theuda told her of what was new, that he was to be one of the Ten.

'It is true? It is done then?' Brightness came opening in her.

He nodded.

'And with the death, I won a freedom,' he said.

'A freedom?'

'Aithne! For so long I had dreamed my dream. Then you lay with Buck that night and it was a darkness for me.'

'Me? I lay with him? What are you saying? I have never lain with a man.' Then her face shaped from puzzlement to laughing. 'No!' she cried. 'It wasn't me – it was Dillo! I asked her so that I could see it. I wanted to know!' And she laughed her delight.

Suddenly the day was spent. A weight of gusting struck through the wood and left them driven against a trunk. A clouded overburdening settled on Theuda. He scraped at the bark with a nail.

'I killed him,' he said quietly. 'I had hate for him and I killed him.'

But Aithne had her laughter still.

'And now you are one of the Ten!'

Theuda turned to her.

'I killed him.'

44

'Soon,' she said, leaning to float it into Theuda's ear. 'Soon comes the feast!'

But he shook his head and had no hearing for her. He was again with the filth of the death.

'My child!' she murmured to herself.

Later, he beat at his skull with his fist. But she had gone back into the wood.

He ran to the river and there above him the wind tore a hole in the clouds. Light of sky showed her: she was moving on quickly towards the holm.

'Aithne!' His mouth was stuffed by the gale.

He ran again. There where she had been, he saw a large hare swimming the river. Her ears were flat; thin light glossed her eye as she went.

'Alphito!' he breathed and stepped back.

And immediately from close by him:

'Theuda!'

'Dillo?'

A vagueness of form was rising from the shade below the bank. The hare had gone. The wind drove with constancy.

'Down here!' she called. 'The wind!'

At the bank foot there was an overhang and deep grass.

'You know these places,' he said in the shelter. 'It is as if they were part of you.'

For a while they were still.

'You have fear in you, Theuda. It is not right.'

He was within himself for a moment. Then:

'Dillo, tell me! The Horn Fellow who is honour, I fear with love. Sun and strength and blood are his – and this I can follow. But there are other things, things of darkness and blind feeling, that are not of him. And these which I cannot know nor understand, I fear. Tell me what they are!'

Dillo fell silent. But finally she answered him:

'You would like to know all by knowing, Theuda. This cannot be. There is the clarity of day; but there is the night too and the weight of shadows. They are about you and are what they are. Of them you may only dream.'

45

And then, from out of her words, a vision of sleep was stalking him. He heard her still: songful in voice and the warmth always close to him. The words she was speaking rose into an ascension of sounds with callings and soft mewlings that prised anguish away. Once she touched him lightly, in a secret way: and he was drifting then, in a ring closed with warmth, unbreathing, secure.

It was the wind backing that stirred him. He was alone.

That night his dream came again, fierce and binding as ever before. There was the bidding to obedience and all the sensing of promise: but still the face was shut off from him. He woke and Aithne's name was there in the night with him.

Horn calls threw him awake next.

He came out of the hut. The sky was just breaking, white fire pressing up from the forest. High overhead, the scrapings of night cloud were sliding away.

He gazed round in wonder. It was Ura.

5

Barring had been put at the entranceway. And dogs too, unfed for days. Movements of the forest brought them up against the tethering, yawping for flesh. The Scaur was a closed place.

Throughout the day, the ale bowls were filled. Fire of oak was always there – for its burning was one of endurance and triumph – and the men were about it, sharers of laughter and of things now gone. Food followed on food and Theuda was urged to it: they would not eat on the second or third days.

As the sun rose over, great heat fell on them out of a wilderness of sky, drawing sweat in streams. But they merely brought more wood to the fire and sent up shouts of challenge, spurring each other further with the ale and with feats of skill.

Theuda's head was back and the hot light was eating his face. There was a jangling with rocking movements behind his eyes and it pleased him. He sucked at the bowl and felt the coolness flow into his chest while heat drove runnels on the skin. Again he drank and as he tipped his head to the sun, an image swung over him, of the faces of the old ones and the axework in the rain long before.

'No!' He fell aside, bowl spewing, and ground his face in the dust. 'No!'

And suddenly his hands were rods of anger, beating, and his throat was churning for ways of speaking his horror. Other hands came to him to hold and there were the voices too, leaning over with the sun's heat and calling sense with repetitions of dismay. But he fought, twisting his head every way to escape from what was clamped to him; and kecked at the words lying half-shaped in his mouth.

A flat-handed clout stopped him and Deor's voice in his ear:

'Theuda, let it be!' Deor was holding him close and propping him with gentle words.

'I . . . I had to!' Theuda spurted. 'I did! I killed but I had to! She told me! To be free!' And he was at the wrestling again, blowing sounds, unable to carry the knowledge.

Deor brought him back slowly.

'Who?' he said. 'Who told you?'

And Theuda, very quietly, now calm:

'I don't know.'

The day went on. The fire and joy soon rose again; even Theuda, though stilled awhile, was laughing. And when the night came and the firelight called them in from the dark, the ale bond strengthened and their love for Saer the Tineman was foremost. They joined together in the old chant and were full of praise for him: for he had the wardenship of their lives and without his passing from them, there could be only failure and decay.

It was late when Saer stood and brought silence on them. Theuda saw the change, with the Men of Scaur putting the ale aside and letting a fierce rigour come into their faces. Down at the entrance, there was a snarling among the dogs; darkly in the forest, an owl called. The feast fire whined and popped around its cavernous heart and, as Saer waited, he was veiled by the oily rise of heat.

He thanked them. As friends of his life and for the day's feasting.

'Tomorrow,' he said and the peace of happiness shone in him, 'tomorrow you shall all be guests of mine.'

Theuda met Kuno with Witu by the huts. All of them had gone to the forest and drunk from the salted water, purging themselves for the rites. Now weakened, they would sleep till the new sun rose.

'Theuda,' said Kuno, coming forward, 'listen to me. You must take care. Corm would find a way of hurting you.'

'He was speaking against you,' said Witu. 'Today, when you fell.'

'Saying what?'

'Oh, there was nothing in it,' answered Kuno hastily. 'He just spoke in a wild way.'

48

'Cynric was his friend from youth,' put in Witu. 'He was saying that you used your powers to bring him to his death.'

Theuda glanced out to the darkness of the forest.

'I have no fear of him,' he said. 'In the fight he would be nothing.'

'He would not fight you,' answered Kuno. 'He has too much cunning for that. He will try and hurt you otherwise.'

The three of them stood silent beneath the stars.

Before he slept, Theuda made his wishes to the Horn Fellow, asking that safekeeping be given to his purpose. For this, he made promise of a boar taken singly.

The second day came on from out of heavy mist. Dawn was unseen, known only slowly by night fading with bird noises striking up blind in the denseness around. Again the horn rang, firmly and swollen with force; and the sound was fell and enormous within the glistening cloud. Soon afterwards, a doe was heard, giving call to her fawn, and this was considered a thing of good boding for them.

Through the mist, they went down to a pool in the stream shortly above where it met the river. With them they had a small boat hollowed from alderwood and this they left secured to the bank. Saer then took from Deor an axe, small and holly-hafted, and cut a sapling of alder. The wood, white inside the tanning bark, bled crimson beneath the keenness of edge. The Men of Scaur stood hushed as the Tineman placed the blooded piece in the boat and laid hands on it.

> Bark red, flower green, twig brown,
> Fire, water and loyal earth,
> The threefold tree.

Then, passing back amid the bird riot, they came up the stream to a spouting fall where boisterously the water smacked at the darkened shelves of rock. At the fall foot, a hole, deeper than could be known, had been bored out by the plummet of the waters. Into this, Saer first, then one by one, they were lowered till they vanished from sight, coming to the air again startled with cold and braced ready for the rites.

49

Above the fall, where the broken woodlands gave over into the forest stretches, they entered a lazy seething in the mist. Up beyond them, the way was spiked, broaches of light shot flat among the turmoils of cloud. Always higher, lodged somewhere in the sun, was a cuckoo.

They were closed off and silent as they went; for now, with the bathing, the course was set and they would not turn till all had been achieved. Once, earlier, Theuda had looked to Kuno with a whisper, asking him the order of things to come; but it had been as if Kuno had not heard. Clearly, a trusting of belief was all: Theuda now saw it so.

Up above, the Scaur stood under open skies.

Now, in the sun, they stripped themselves and wore only the cloth. Once more they went from the Scaur but upwards further to the sacred ground where the pines grew thick, walling in a stretch of grass. Here twelve stones stood in a ring about a planted trunk, an oak axe-trimmed to a flat fork shape; and before this was the great lying stone. Behind the trunk and out beyond the ring, a holly grew, sturdy and shining dark.

They had come with oaken brands and, for the keeping of strength, they went first to build the new fire. Around its burning they then gathered and the pouch was given. The berry growths were tough and scorching to the tongue.

Saer himself sat against the lying stone; the others each took a stone of the ring though Deor the tanist, who was of the Tineman yet not of him, who was to be apart, beyond the round of force, both protector of the Tineman's unguarded back and still his final, hidden enemy – Deor went to his allotted place beneath the holly tree.

Theuda watched. His back was straight and the stone against him was shadow cold. The ring was firm with silence and there was only the living fire and elsewhere, far and hidden, the mewing of buzzards. He let his eyes move about. There was no stirring at the stones: each was seeing only himself and following the strength that would grow out of their joined presence. Everywhere, faces were flat with absence.

He chewed long at the berries, thinking to make juice against the fieriness. The taste was bitter and old. He held them in his mouth listlessly and made patterns of their turning on his tongue. It was a time for waiting.

'One, only one!' a voice said later out of somewhere. And with that the pouch landed by him.

He looked round at the speaker but did not know him. The new berry he chewed with a mute fury, crunching and gnawing in his haste. The burning had tailed off; for a warmth was in him everywhere now. He took in breath deeply and snorted it away again.

A humming had started and it was in the fire. He joined with it, holding low, and his eyes were closed. There was a full swarming of bees in his mouth: so he spoke the shape of words with his lips and immediately a stream of bees flowed out. It pleased him this and he spoke more shapes around the humming and then others were doing it too so that waves and forms grew in the sound and crowded the echoes in his head.

But then, of a sudden, fear was speaking to him. It made him straggle a bit, hang back from what was on the move. And at this, his eyes were open again and he was looking round at them all, his chin sagging as if under a dead weight.

But the Men of Scaur were no longer as he knew them! The features were theirs but on men other than them, outlanders who must now hold power.

Oh, springes had taken him! Trickery! Free, to get free, to cover!

He made fights with his legs, pushed against the stone, made for rising. Gasps shot from him, wetness ran hot on his thigh, an eye was puckering.

'Theuda! The—uda!' The voice was of a friend and came perhaps from inside him. The trees rocked with it. 'The ring, Theuda! It needs you!'

Theuda slid back. A face was hanging before him.

'Berry!' said Theuda, sullen with his fear. 'Give me a berry!'

'No!' The face spoke. 'Later. They are strong.'

'I cannot! I am lost!'

'Let go! Remember – you are here for the god. Let him guide you!'

'I cannot!'

'You can! Believe!'

And fingertips, snow cool, placed a light pressure to his temples. Startled, Theuda stilled.

The humming held its rhythms about him and the touch of fingers seemed always there. With it, Theuda was slowing, coming out to a level; and this falling was to a state which stood beyond fear.

By now, the sun was towards its peak.

Later, he noticed that the humming had stopped. His head was back on the stone but he could tell that there was movement about. Darkness crossed the sun and a voice came gathering speed from afar.

'Here!' And berries dropped into his mouth.

Laughter of ease guggled in him. Then the drifting took him again; but only shortly for he passed through this to a starkness where he perceived everything with wonder. And his wonder came from him in a sharp cry for he saw then in the ring a buck, reared up, stroking the air.

'The Horn Fellow!' His words breathed themselves.

The buck was parading. When it stood before him, Theuda wanted to speak his praise; but the dumbness of awe tied him. He sat bowed, the trembles skittering on his shoulders as the great beast snouted and pawed the ground. When it had passed round the full ring, the buck went from them.

The sun was high and going over: the sky bare and eaten out white by heat. Harshly the light fired down and in the forest edges there was much creeping to shade. In the ring though, they sat brazened beneath the sun. Now an incantation had set up, a pauseless coil form of sounds mouthed flat that brought binding and effacement. It drew steadily, leading Theuda always in. Stone rigid with eyes that gaped, he sat locked within the sound play; and before him, in the fire, were bucks, forked shapes and flicker fast the movement of hoofs.

Fierce heat later fell to warmth. Twice since noon the berry pouch had gone to the ring and the power had held the chant unbroken. But lastly, at the sun's midfall, Theuda felt the stream force of the ring suddenly go faltering. Then too the chant was pierced and finally it gave way and was gone altogether.

Everything fell from beneath him: there was only deadening and the spaces of void. His head swung and he clutched forward at the ground. But he was drawn up short from this as a shout went rising around him, delight and ferociousness together.

There, back in the ring, was the buck, head high; and with it a red-haired man who was calling success and promise to them, telling them that the great pairing had been made. He told them how he had waited at the opening, up on the peaks, and had watched as the god went down the dark ways to Alphito. Beneath an eagle rising he had waited – an omen of omens – and then had been witness to the god's glory returning from the depths.

At this, the shouts arose again and the men were leaving the stones to forgather. Theuda found his legs strong and a calm in his chest that made breathing unnoticed. He ran in too and received the bowl: cool and clear it was and he emptied it swiftly. They all drank from it and so too was the buck given to eat. Then they took burning logs from the fire so that twin flames should stand in the ring.

When both fires burned up strongly, the buck ate again and then of a sudden was moving off at a stagger, its head fighting the weight of horn. Theuda watched it and was curious.

But now too he was feeling his body grow immense in strength and a recklessness bursting violent in him that would have had him cry out. He stamped a bit and beat his fist on his thigh. And then there was noise and others were running and he was helping them draw the buck to the oak trunk. Upright they pulled him and soon thongs of osier bound him about the oak by the joining of hoofs and neck.

Now cries and the bellowing of excitement echoed on the sacred ground and the men had taken sticks and were ringing the oak and striking hard at the buck. The blows had fury in them and no pausing so that soon the buck hung, its life showing just in the lightest of breathing. Then a knife was taken and cuts made and by this the skin was flayed away.

Shouts rose.

Somebody was pushing at Theuda. Hands came past and made sharp movements at the buck's eyes; then went again. Theuda peered forward at the red weeping of the holes. He howled and tried to bite at the smooth flesh; but in the roaring, arms pulled him off and then another went past him with the knife. Ducked down and grasping went the man: twice gashed his knife and then, with his turning to the crowd, the blue of sky showed strong behind the male parts held high.

Theuda shook and was a dog barking. He bounded in again to help others draw the hindquarters outwards from the oak and kept them propped under as the mistletoe stake went in sleekly at the vent. With the stick came gore spouting; and bubblings and dark matter.

Cut down, the carcase was put out on the lying stone. There before them it was, eye-blind and shattered, and a respect held them. But then the blade had fallen and there was the bowl below the neck and blood well-springing as the head was carried aside.

The bowl cast its blood upwards out of sight into the sun. When the thick rain covered them then joy burst. They touched at it, smeared and pressed it, held against each other: for now there was in them sheer gladness – their hopes of renewal had been brought about.

Again the shaking was in Theuda. And in among the wild noises, his dog calls grew to the troating of bucks, head thrust with the swinging of eyes. He saw and still he knew them all without recognition yet now he was part of them complete: the blood death was their sharing, together they had come to a meeting of truths. Now they knew that vigour and plenty would come in for them. And the brilliance of his gladness for it was tearing him open.

Some slaked themselves with the cooling drink; others were

working the fires for the roasting of the flesh. Theuda had an axe and it was for him to split the oak trunk for its burning. Men spoke and chanted, sun struck at the business of blades and the fire hearts were pulsing.

The limbs crisped well. Fat sprang in the flames with wasp noises and bursts; richness was on the air for the waiting men. A fist of pigeons opened out over and heads reeled with the light.

Theuda took a strip of thigh. When all had meat, they formed the necessary shape about the fires, loops crossing, and began to move. The great deed had been done; the achieving was theirs. The sun was low but now there was only the closure and the knowledge of it loosed the day-long severeness from them. They were moving then running; chanting turned to howls and a fury of rejoicing. Teeth tore into the flesh with juices dribbling and as they gave shouts they were stamping their excitement, dust and ash and blood together. Long beyond the eating of the flesh, they made the coiling runs about the fires for the cooling drink had given them the strength; and so still they sped, flecked and gape-eyed, as the sun came lowering on to the trees.

The youngest and the newest had been sent.

Below the blood sky, the deeps of the forest were thickening into dusk. Warmth smouldered in the open ways but dankness of night grew around the bushes' roots. Standing high out from the fallen day, the taloned moon presided.

They came down slowly, in silence, Theuda leading Kuno who bore the basket. They were voided, hollowed to utterness by the rites: now, with the loudness still ringing through them, they moved only on the strength of trust. There was not even talking in them; for bloodlessness and awe of what they were about was cramping them. Their task was fearful and solemn.

The fires had sprung up and fallen away again with the last remains of the sacrifice before the basket was secured and given over to the two men. Water lightly salted was taken to restore; then, as the earliest of the stars took up stands over the forest, Theuda and Kuno had heard the word and so gone forth from the sacred ground, downwards alone.

Theuda's face was cold. He carried hurting, bruising in him that was of a battling to recall and its refusal; he was swithering among the dreams of deeds. Terror and wonder standing close by in him drew him powerlessly on.

Now they came through the middle forest, lost from the heights, still far from the riverland. Only the stepping of their feet and the stream's work down below them in the growth of night were heard. The beasts were gone and it was as if only mourning were there.

There was moonlight in the stream when they came to it. And against the gleam, the small boat nodding. They gathered the drooping leaves off the bank and made a lining for the boat with them. On these, with a last reverence, they placed Saer's head and his man's parts; then cut the boat loose to the broad current. It ran away, crossing the light, and was gone beneath the overhang of trees.

Sunfall had seen them gather there. Now the soft threads of their singing lay among the lamps upon the river skin while the line they had formed, lower down in the shallows between holm and bank, swayed on the brink of the darkness. Birds of the night and a meeting of bats broke cover over them, underlit in dimness; and the women themselves, they too gleamed dully with the oiling as they stood to their waists in the sloth of the waters.

By movement and the ebb of shadows, the banded ones were seen, holding the centre stream. With them, makers of the line, were the other women, those who had been to the mountain in years before. Some of these had the tenfold scorings of blood on them, cut across the flesh; and so too elsewhere the crescents, burnt and stained in for glory.

The singing was resolute yet was shot through with calls of yearning. Bodies leaned, stretching forward upriver to what was unknown, out beyond the lamps. When the moon stood up from between the hills and the water mass caught a touch of its whiteness, a surging of cries came, wonder and the heightening of hope together. But soon again it was gone, the moon worked over by the drift of night cloud. Then it was that darkness was heavier and the flutter glow yellowing into weakness; and so the voices rose, strengthened by the pitch of their longing.

Lamplight still held when the shout came. It broke out against rhythm from the far edge of the line and with it, at once, the singing tailed into nothingness. A fish sprang and stunned flatly down in the quiet that had come in. All eyes were striving.

'There!' the young voice cried. 'There!'

And then, as the shape came up to the first of the lamps, new shouts joined. Quickly sound piled and was building; and arms were pointing for already the boat was deep among the lamps. But of a sudden the great sound was turned for women had started the hymning of the boat, strict and slow. The power of shouting fell away and voices broke into the two parts of the ritual singing, each half of the river line giving answer to the other as the boat came on down to them. A calm of sureness was with them now and their faces were brightened with promise.

It reached them then, there in the midstream where the banded ones were. The line closed in, singing still but now fierce in throat. They gloried in the sight of the boat: it had come to them, to them alone. And so the banded ones were first and then the others by turns. With the singing raised to beating shouts, an angry joy, they came to the boat and ate.

Blossom of hawthorn had made it. The man took and rubbed their palms with it; then, laughing, brought themselves into their dreaming, faces down into hands. There were silences and oaths.

Theuda too went down to his hands, curious for it. Daylight closed off and his breath drawn in brought him on the instant the smell of the clovenness of women. The sun shining elsewhere sent through his hands delicate flowering pink of flesh

57

and dewiness of warmth. Surprise had him breathe and then again. He was burrowing at the smell with his face and his elbows were pressing down on the eagerness of his yard. Of a sudden, it was as if possession had to be his and in this there was a fury of need that gave him fixity and oxen might. He was hungering and must take.

His name was spoken but he would not hear it. It came again, across his intentness, and then they were throwing pebbles at him too. When he looked up, there was a snarl in his face and they were nodding, hung about with smiles. He snarled a bit more but then it was beginning to leave him. He let it go and threw his laugh in with theirs, rolling over in the sunlight. The clear heat stamped on his groin.

They were high, out above the forest, the Ten. The tanist, with Eudo and Witu, had seen them go from the Scaur as the sun passed down from its heights. Water had cleansed them and their bodies were smooth. From the Scaur, they had taken the ancient way till the pines began to stand thin; and from there they had gone by goat trails upwards towards the comb of rock that held the highest ridge. Now from the flag of stone where they sat, all things were to be seen. Over at the comb's foot, there was movement.

They drank lazily but with care. They talked too but as the day shortened, the stillnesses began to come on them and they found themselves given up to silence. Tails of a sky wind made curls on the rock and this they knew was the god flowing among them. And so as the sun fell, they were gradually drawn from idleness of talk into the strengthening quiet. They knew of the night to come and their laughter, a warding of fear, was bringing them over into the rise of mystery.

Afterlight of day stood above as the Ten came along the ridge. Uhtred, as the oldest, was leading them in. He had spoken words for their fortune and had given each to taste as appointed. Then they had gone from the rock and made towards the pricks of light by the comb.

And already, from the tasting, the change was in them. Theuda felt lightness buoy him as an awakening. He traced each press and spring of muscle as he stepped and the mere chancing of his hand against his thigh brought a tremor to him. And so too it had begun to seem to him that he was alone. The others, his friends, paced along with him and he knew them there; yet an enormousness of self ruled him. He, only he bore the right of need! His was to be the covering . . . ! And he snuffled at his hand and drummed with his feet as he went. The thin colouring overhead soared from him in his dizziness.

At the comb, small fires were burning and banks of fuel lay in by the rock. The women, hooded and turned from the approach of the men, stood about the fires and there was silence among them and no moving. A fearsomeness hung over this meeting, there far out on the open ridge. Theuda saw it so and was chilled. Yet he came on in with the men, still quickened with his lust.

But then he was stumbling, heart held, as mute shrieks came up from the women. Bat noises swarmed. Without Uhtred leading, hesitation would surely have tripped and tied the men. Yet Uhtred was walking still and they were following; while the high racketing was all about them in the dusk.

Then Uhtred was walking into the rock and the bats were following. Theuda's head twisted about and he would have cried out warnings. But suddenly the wall of the rock comb had taken Uhtred: head dropped, he had plunged forward and was quite gone. And then the others too. And, with the massed shriekings closing behind him, horror was building into a quailing of heart in Theuda. But then he saw it; and how Leudi, before him, had stepped down and ducked himself under it, the low arching at the comb foot.

Theuda had no choice.

'It is to be!' he thought and was gone under, with the darkness and the rock scraping his back.

He came up and was blind. A pace forward into his blindness and flesh met him.

'Wait a while!' a voice hushed back at him.

Outside, the bats had settled. Now crackling of fires was beginning there.

Theuda screwed his eyes against the hood of dark. He could hear the others close by – the breathing and the secret words to the god – and his heart found some settling. From the corner of his eyes he peered and time passing showed a soft glory growing, a light waxen and vague. He reached out to hold it but it was beyond. And against this glimmering, a shoulder, a head, gradually the Ten. It was then that he knew the light was far and that much that was hidden and unsure lay between. But in the very knowing, he was ready: for venturing in the god's name was all. Roaring of fires stood behind: wonders lay ahead unknown.

And then they were moving. Forward slowly, by touch and hope, they went. The way was smooth to the foot and was rising beneath them. Out of somewhere that was without place, rods of metal were touching lightly together. The air shivered with their sound and it set a creeping of pleasure upon the men.

And so too the light began to stir, a swaying between growth and fading; and they blinked at this crazing of the dark. Then, from the rise, they were looking down into new blackenings. The light had wavered further and was going from them and dimming, fast within a narrow cleaving of the rock. So haste drove them towards it, down in soft padding pursuit; and then they were thrusting along the cleft, barking arms on the narrowness with sand lying fine and cool underfoot. Each step of their going had turns in it, with rock prowing out into bulges that brought them to confusion.

Then, from the cleft's deep beyond, it seemed to them that the light had fixed. A flaring of it opened up across the height of the walls above but then went out altogether. The rod sounds too: so that the Ten found themselves taken in the toils, by stilled night and the mazes of the way.

Throats tightened against breath, mouths hung and each ear was leaning out into the darkness. Then:

'Uhtred!'

'What?'

'What now?'

'We wait. It is for them to guide.'

Theuda's fingers were at his ribs, scratching lightly. His eyelids quivered, almost to closing, and he made bites at his lip. His hand was up and with the smelling, all his hungering and sureness was with him as before. He knocked his head in pleasure against the rock.

Surprise took them as a spill of light entered the cleft behind. And a call, willowing, that played around itself. And now, in their going, it was Theuda leading and his body was strong and he knowing that others must follow as they willed. When a side opening lay brightened, he was climbing; and the light was suddenly in a hole and he would crush his way through and when he did there was the drift of warmth and flowers and he was falling.

Leudi was landing beside him as Theuda drew himself off the slope. But Theuda saw neither him nor even the others as they came for already he was far in his wonder.

Ten were the women holding the cave. They stood in their nakedness, bone-bald and with their faces chalked white as the moon. Angered coilings of patterns covered them on breast and belly and about them rose sweetness of the woods from flowers laid deep in layers. Their eyes, from within the darkening of stain, looked up at the men and were weighted and sharp: attack was in them yet with promise too.

Now the women began to gesture and were giving out long churrings like goatsuckers far off. Their bodies were in movement and the stained shapes flowed snaking on them, wave over wave. And so the men began to come to them.

Theuda had looked for Aithne. But now he was seeing only the ripple of the snakes among breasts that belled and the haunches playing slowly in the shadows.

The white faces kept firm, with eyes that started with immensity and were sightless. Theuda made towards one who was softly fleshed but sharp in features. He stood with her, watching her moving body and was reaching out when somewhere there were the rods touching again and then the light went from the cave.

A hand seized his arm.

'Me – not her!' a violence blew into his ear.

Theuda made to break free but another hand clutched his yard and put nails with threats at the edge of his balls. He stood quiet.

Now the dimness showed up small cuppings of light, scattered about in the cavern. When the hand freed him, he went gently led to a recess beyond, where flowers were a bed.

It was both dark and light there. Elsewhere already, among the sounding rods, was laughter and busy silence.

Now Theuda could see but the shape of her.

'Aithne?'

The face of the moon came flashing and a bite caught him quickly on the chest. She sprang back, breathing a smile, but he was fast and bore her down. Beneath them, the flowers broke and a misting of summer smells opened about.

There was fighting in them, brute need and the will for taking. Teeth clashed and mouth juices spread on face and neck. She tore at him, drawing nets of blood over him with her nails. And he, tonguing her and sucking, was lifting from her body's skin the sweet fruit-stain shapes; was foraging, nibbling, finding entrance everywhere. Snarlings rolled in him and she would draw in hissings and give the steady, untuned sounds of pleasure. And then he turned down on her and wildness came into him with mouth and hand among the sappy pungencies of opening and petalled flowers.

The cavern was resonant with coupling. Theuda and the river girl were borne on by it, as by a flood; but suddenly, the storming in Theuda was touched upon by the image of the godhead and all the promise of his dream. He drew back and, in his pausing, spoke her name. Then he brought her round and upped her hips; and with the softness of might, he made his way into her. She piped a cry with the blood but went with him in his moving. Long-drawn the rhythm they made while he pulled and clawed upon her back and her buttocks that came cool to his thighs and she biting among the flowers.

And so, with a secret call to the god, he gave himself over

and made on, brought to a ram of strength; and lastly as he drove, she gave a cry for what was to be hers.

Yet there was no quenching. Later and again, it livened in them and they lay cast together, loosing themselves and now with laughing pleasure. And then it was, in their peace, that Aithne spoke to him:

'You must leave me now or they will see.' And to him rising, a whisper: 'Theuda – all this has been as it was set. And there is gladness in this for me. For now it will be as I have hoped – I am sure of it!'

Then she gave him to taste and so he went from her, rejoicing for his dream. Yet already the greed was in him again and he went into the cavern prowling and found himself a woman alone.

Throughout that night, the men passed among the women, tasting often to bring up the vigour. The women lay for them in the lairs, waiting and watching, faces white in darkness and lamplight glistening harshly in flickerless eyes. Theuda lost all knowledge of himself and there was only the frenzy of need drawing him on into the corners and the twine of the snakes. Words did not come: it was the sounds of the rut and the occasional touching of rods that held the air.

Once, as he was resting up against breasts slicked with sweat, he heard noises and hurrying; and then stifled words that were nothing yet had vastness in the maw of the night. And when, later, he went back with his longing to Aithne, there was only shadows and the crushed matting of flowers.

With the fading of the night, lights guided the Ten back to the outer cave. From there, by the entrance arch, they came stooping and broke way up across the long watchfires, now abandoned to ashen whiteness; and then up again into the sharp breezes of dawn. There, weakened and chill, they stood and clasped one another before taking to the track that made down over rock and scree towards the forest edge far below.

6

And Deor was Tineman.

In the breathless stretching of days that came in after the feast, the achievement of belief struck up happiness among the Men of Scaur. Yet this was broken into; for at the greeting of the incomer, discontent rose as a dark growth in their midst.

He called himself Acur, the new one, and was sharp-boned. His eyes moved tightly and though his mouth was no more than a gash, his voice was a cave. One of the skills he had was as a maker of bird sounds: in the Scaur he was often to be heard calling to the birds out in the forest.

To Theuda, Acur seemed merely oversure; but some of the others held differently.

The three fleshmen sat with Theuda by night.

'He is one of theirs, the women. That is what we say.' It was Beohrt speaking.

'You can tell,' said Romac. 'He stands with us and even has a smile on his face – but his words are wrong.'

'Yes and there is always an edge of sneering in his speech.'

Theuda looked across at Acur, gaunt by the wall of night beyond the fire.

'Romac, the other day you said they were planning something.'

Romac, all stoat face and wiriness, looked at Theuda.

'That you had heard things,' coaxed Theuda.

Romac nodded slowly.

'Ead,' he said, 'the tall one who wears the white sow's head – she and those with her would like to change the way of things.'

'She talks of the women coming here to the Scaur,' put in

Fer. 'She says that their being kept from it has long been a thing of offence to them. She would like us to believe that they could be of use to us here.'

Beohrt broke out with a huff of scorn.

'And the holm?' asked Theuda. 'Would they want us to go there?'

Romac shrugged.

'There was no talk of that.'

'Madness!' said Beohrt. 'I tell you, it is all madness.'

And so it passed. But in the days that came, Acur slowly grew to find acceptance with the Men of Scaur. Other than those moments, early of an evening, when he was to be seen at the edge of the Scaur making his trills and whistles out over the listening forest, most of his time he spent with Corm; and Corm, dull and silent since Cynric's death, brightened with it and a new eagerness came into his face. It was also noticed how Corm was now busying himself with certain of the men. At the time, the others saw nothing amiss in this; but soon after, when suddenly there arose a nursling spirit of dissent in the Scaur, they believed they knew why.

When this happened, Deor called the men together and spoke to them of his sorrow.

'My friends! Men of Scaur!' he began and he spoke with weight. 'All last night I stood watch with the stars in my grief. For in these my first days as Tineman, I have found here amongst us an embittering and a gall growth in our trust. And I tell you this: the Scaur will stand nothing of such discord – closeness alone can keep our heart in strength. As one of you and as a friend till death, I say this.' And anger of command then rose in his voice. 'As Tineman, I now call upon your oaths for the truth! It must live no longer, this thing! It must be shaped in words and put away!' Then he turned. 'Eudo, will you speak for what is being voiced in secrecy?'

And in answer, Eudo came forward, smith-strong and darkly. He spoke up to all and was clear in his words.

'It is true! It is as Deor says: before all, the Scaur's strength must be held.' Then he paused and his voice lowered: 'Being mindful of my oath for the truth, I must say that there are those in the Scaur who will not see the ways forward. And, in my opinion, when men can only stare back at what has been then weakness has come creeping in.'

But a voice burst in:

'What has been is right! This has always been so!'

'No! Strength allows for change!' called back Eudo. 'To stay still is to begin to die!'

Murmured sounds rose and covered him. And with them the sun was driving out from the clouds and breaking upon the pines. A breeze blew.

'Who has been speaking to you, Eudo?' shouted Kuno.

'Is it Corm, I wonder?' followed Romac. 'Or Acur?'

'I speak with all and with no one!' barked Eudo. 'My words belong to me alone!'

Then Deor called silence on them.

'Will no man speak the clear truth? I have no joy in this squalling of vixens.'

No voice answered him. It was Theuda who finally spoke up.

'The women of the holm would come visiting here. They say that they could be of use to us. And there are some among us who would have it so.'

Deor's eyes were fixed beneath a brow of creases.

'To the Scaur? And you, Eudo, you are one of these?'

'Deor, I am. I can see no harm in it. What wrong could they do us? Are we not men and so able . . .?'

'Fool! You fool!' roared Beohrt. 'Can you not see? They would use it to weaken us. To let them would be to seek disaster. They are women!'

'He is right! Beohrt is right!' called Romac. And echoes came from Fer and Kuno.

But now suddenly Brun and Witu were standing by Eudo and throwing jeers back at them. And then shouts were lancing up everywhere. It was only when order had been called on the noise that Corm came sidling out to the middle.

'On my oath,' he said, soft of voice and looking round out

of a face disguised, 'on my oath, I must count myself with those who would see the women here. What threat could there be in this? Indeed, might it not be something of a strengthening?

'But we should hear what everyone has to say on this. The Tineman and his men by right hold silence till last – but every other, being bound by his oath, must declare himself or be thought a coward and so forfeit his power of right. Has Theuda, friend and wordmaster, forgotten this?' And with that, he turned with eyebrows arching to Theuda and held still.

A hawk, blind-mad in pursuit, went past, souse down the cliff. Drops of rain pipped lightly, sun shone and the sky above was clear of cloud. Away below, a doe called pinched wheezes to her fawn. All this in the instant as the coils were drawn up tight within Theuda. He shook his head and blew down his nose to beat back the swell and the shaking; he stood firm and forced the paces of reason on himself. Then he looked at Corm and the words rose stinging out of him:

> Rot stinks sweet;
> Black hang the flies.
> Theirs is the feeding:
> We shall not pause
> To scatter them.

Brun and Witu sprang and were quickly with Corm. Slow fester of feeling had burst and there was a din growing of shouts as the fleshmen in return came up by Theuda. Gestures of fight were made: only Theuda and Corm were still, holding the touch of eyes, Corm smiling.

But Deor would not have it so. He strode in, face flashing, and at the raise of his spear, the cries were draining from the air.

'Stop this!' he called. 'Silence! Men of Scaur, hear me now! This I tell you: that so long as the power is with me, there shall be no such whelp-snarling here amongst us. Let this be closed – for I put the say of the Tineman and his men with those who would hold to the ways of old. The women shall not come here. Such a thing is not to be thought of.'

And thus again it was past. Once more there was only the procession of days when the heat hung long beneath the forest towers and the great clouds of summer made their progress slowly on the blue. Rain came but little and the earth was made into crack forms and dustiness.

Once, during these dying days of the Oakmonth, Theuda came by himself to the stream, there where he and Kuno had put the feast boat to the waters. The need for closeness with himself had been strong within him since the days of Ura and that morning he had startled from sleep and gone straight from the Scaur to find the secrecy of the woods.

Birdsong was all in the heights at that hour. The stream ran low and under the massing leaf-burst of bushes, shadow and black earth were rank. Going down from the Scaur, Theuda had had no knowledge of intent. Blind urging alone had led him and even now it held him there as he stood before the sleeking waters with eyes stilled in horror. And then suddenly he had fallen and was knee-bent in the cool grasses, brought down by fear of himself and the deeds of the feasting days. Knuckles ridged and were pale about a stem of tree; and grim awe was gathering fury in him and laying quavers in his limbs. Dog snaps and a throttling in the gullet rose from him and his eyes began to whiten.

'Theuda!'

Deor's call from above was whispered loud. And with it he was making speed on the slopes.

'Theuda!' He took Theuda in his arms and felt the death cold against him, rocklike. 'Theuda, it is me, Deor!' And then, on his shoulder, the noises went out and there was only the unbreathing and the weight.

So Deor gave the faith of warmth. Theuda at last came free and let himself be led. Together they turned from the stream and rose away with the silence of friends into the higher woods towards the sun.

All that day they walked, passing over into new valleys of

the forest and again beyond till the Scaur lay remote and hidden from them. In the late heat of the sun, they went up to where the tree growth was split open by paps of rock and so began to scale the heights. Hard by the length of a fluting fall they rose, webbed by moistening and the scream of birds; and then above they turned for the peak. There in a cave they made their fire and talked together below the cusps of the floating moon.

Through the length of the sun's going, Theuda had had no words in him. But now, by the spit of fire high in the dark places, the words came and to him Deor gave the solace of his understanding. It was later, as the last of the pain was eased from him, that Theuda felt the strength of new love for Deor. It stood shining in the firelight of his eyes and the manner of his head; it was in the movement of hands and all the silences between. And so too it was with Deor. Words of this were not: joy of it was greater so.

The fullness of night swelled upon the hills below. Stars held appointedly their distant stands. Slowly, the embering was growing within the fire.

For three days they were together from the Scaur. For three days they stood upon the hills, there where the hot light made its fusings with the wind. Pathwork they followed on to ridges by boulder and pinnacle point, travelling always with speed, and there was the fire of spirit with them in their going. Unseamed walls of rock stood beneath the hang of great birds as the two passed; there was pebble clatter of goats ringing over the shadowing of rift; and, occasionally, prickles of softness upon them, spray drawn up from a fall of the slopes.

Such was their going in those days of the sun, with all of pleasure and strength. By night, when starlight was still, they sat there in the heights together, speaking of belief and the wonder of the hunt, of the blood death's living force and all the mastery of the Horn Fellow himself. And with this, so too was the pledging of friends.

69

Ahead of the searchers came the dogs, bursting on the two with fierceness of recognition and ducking down to paw up in greeting. The forest opening was massed with their cries.

'We thought you gone from us,' said Kuno in reproach as he drew the dogs in.

'Gone from you?' said Deor sharply. 'I am the Tineman. How should I go from you?'

'You were away three days without word,' replied Kuno just as quickly. 'We were not to know.'

Closeness of love and all the anguish of it showed in this crossing of words.

But now the others came and gave their greeting too. Corm, who had been hanging back, pushed through to Deor. From his kneeling, he spoke:

'The Scaur has its heart of strength again and we give our thanks for this.' This loudly, for the hearing of all. Then, in glancing up and so quietly: 'Yet would it not be well for the Tineman's strength to be put in trust when he is away? All know that troubles have been with us, that there is less of sureness than before.' He paused. 'Men say it would be good to have a tanist named.'

Then there was silence with birdcalls and the sneeze of a dog. Deor's face said nothing. He was looking at Corm.

'Corm, men also know that each thing chooses its own time. There is no choosing it, not for any man, neither Tineman nor otherwise.' This was Deor's reply. And he raised Corm up but would not speak further with him.

That night, when there was quiet laughter and drinking in pleasure, Theuda spat his food from him. Blood ran upon his chin, a gum was sliced: there in the mess of meat and meal, flecks of metal starred in the light of the torches.

Corm was nowhere.

7

From up on the rockfall, Theuda watched her come ashore.

Sunfire had softened as the Hollymonth opened out. Then clouds of drizzling had come sinking down and settled. Now, in the days after, there was all the gentleness of dripping with scatter tufts of cloud hanging in the trees; and below, an underworld with darkness and lurking.

The rocks were wet and tried to escape from his feet as he came quickly down.

'Dillo! Wait!'

And she turned, otter-sleek with the river; and as she knew his face, she did not want to. Hurriedly she made off from him and her loping had swiftness concealed in it so that he had to strive hard to cut her from her course.

'Dillo! We must talk!' The words came spewing through gasps. Now he had her by the arm but she was bending her head from him. 'Dillo, what is it? Why are you so?'

The sky hung low; the river ran. Slowly the breathing slackened. But he did not loosen his hold.

'Dillo! Listen to me! It is Aithne – I am worried for her. I have dreamed things, things full of hurt.'

But now, at this, Dillo was tugging again, leaning further to the river. Anger bounded up in Theuda and he tore her round. He saw her eyes and they were dark fruits bursting. She was shaking her head.

'You know something! Tell me, Dillo!'

But the head still swung and her lips made a line out of firmness.

'Gah!' Theuda threw down her arm and turned for the holm.

'No!' The bolt of her cry sank deeply into him. Then to

him more softly: 'Theuda, no! It is too late.'

For a moment, he stared at the grief in her face: and then he had gone. Power of fear gave him the flight of birds of the hunt, breath drawing long, sinuous the thews as his feet fled on the grasses.

Aithne! Air whistling by teeth carried her name and again; his heart knocking not by effort but for her beauty and all the dreaming of his life. He would find her and safe, he was sure: yet Dillo's eyes seen still made him gather himself further into his speed, strides opening, arms punching free, always streaming.

Aithne!

The holm was close but was held in mist. He slowed and stretched out with his hearing to the river. But the slip-slap at the bank was just the border of nothingness. So he waited; and then by stages the holm was unsheathed.

It was a gagged whisper at first and then a goaded bull roar:

'Aithne!'

For at the island's point she was, white even on the paleness of mist. She was high, the height of two men from the ground, offered up to the sky, and she stood quite still. When he screamed for her, there came nothing for no answering was left in her. He saw her fairness of head propped sideways by the stake that peeped out by her neck. Gore clung to it lower where she held it with her thighs.

He stood half-foundered in the river, babbled mutings on his lips, and made plucks at his hair. Rumble of moans played up from his belly and pulses jerked at his back. The river slid on past him: always the thing on the holm was there.

Later, by low light, it was somehow and elsewhere that he found himself. He let himself rise, coming up from out of the chill deep to feed on the air. Current strands were all about him and an increase of drizzling hung cloaks upon the water world. He mouthed slowly upwards and then sank back by stages into the dark silences where there was only the prickling of bubble breath and a refuge from himself and from things beyond his bearing. Now he had mind for nothing: the cradle strength of the river held him and would take him at its will.

Mist came gathering low as the day fell and, among it, once and again, he heard a drifting of his name. It was nothing to him however and he turned from it. But soon it was speaking close into his ear.

'Theuda, come!'

'She is dead.'

'But come! Drowning will not bring her to you again.'

'She is dead. They killed her.'

'Theuda, you must have strength and know it as it is. Only then can you live.'

'Aithne! Aithne is dead.'

The voice stood off a while. Later though, it came again, hushed in a breath.

'Theuda!'

And with that, the rippling was swallowed into the river and fingers touched him lightly. A line closed on him to his armpits; but then slackened off. He let it be.

Again he lay alone beneath the mist.

He was in dreams of long ago. They hung with him, turning on the edge of the river's stream, warm with light and breast softness, with safety against the howl and the fearsome claws waiting. His lips were shaped at the mist as if teating and his eyes slept in his head with the dreams. Even when the water burbled about him as he was moved in from the stream, he lolled and was as if mindless of it.

Then mud earth was soothing against his leg and the line was holding taut. Hands came; and, letting them take him, so did he come once more to the land, stun-stupid and weak.

For a length of days, there was only lifelessness and blurting in Theuda. Sleep spared him much; but even so he would return breaking from it with eyes swollen and a skin slimed over with sweat. No talking came to him in those shapeless days; but at last, as the sun made on towards the meeting of the Holly- and the Hazelmonths, he turned his head and looked at Dillo.

'Have I been here long?'

She nodded.

'There was no strength in you,' she said.

For a while, he lay back in his silence. Smoke strove about Dillo's head and she was still.

Then, in the quietness:

'But why? Why, Dillo?'

Dillo stroked life into the fire. Outside, it had broken into rain.

Then she gave him to drink and he sucked at the dark bowl with an anger of misery. Dillo sat across from him with her stillness and the seeing was in her eyes.

'Aithne!' he murmured. And so gradually the waking sleep came on him.

'You will know of Ead,' began Dillo and her voice was low and her words woven without edge. 'She has long been hardened in herself and full of anger. Between her and me, there was never friendship; but for Aithne and her beauty, she truly had the hatred of envy.'

In her pausing, the rain was heard steady at the lair mouth.

Then, in the chanting of her words, Dillo told of it. How, in the days before Ura, Aithne had come to her in search of help. For Ead, she had said, was penning her about with threats and putting pitfalls of questions in her path. Did Dillo not have a way for it, to shackle Ead, just till the feast was past? And Dillo, so moved, had given the girl a mixture, a few drops of which would set a body tight-rigid for a daylong span.

Ura had passed. And then, on the day of the moon, but six days back, Aithne had come to her again – but now weighted down with her secret.

For the truth had been all otherwise, were then Aithne's words to Dillo. And so; for now she told how the draught had been not for Ead but for herself. On the mountain, once she had been with Theuda, then she meant to take it. For it was a

74

child she wanted: not the god's child but one made with Theuda alone and he a wordspeaker. Such was her plan and so it had been. There in the flower-heavy darkness of the cave, she had taken the drops and soon after had been borne back to the holm as if dead.

Hearing this, coldness of fear had come over Dillo. For she, as did all the women of the holm, she knew well the word of the law – that a woman, going to the cave and coupling with one man alone, that woman must die. There was no choice: it must be so. For the men children born of the feast, those who might hope one day to be of the Scaur, they were to be sons of the Horn Fellow's power and not of a man.

And so it was. For later Dillo had heard that Ead had somehow come to the truth of things and had called for the exacting of the law. Judgement was given and Aithne was duly handed over to her fate. The ritual of the death was old and showed to all the way in which such an unholy seeding must end.

Theuda stayed on with Dillo of the Bank and gathered himself. Then, beneath a dawn sky strewn with winds, he touched her and gave his thanks. As he turned up towards the woods, he saw below him the river skin crimped shivering; and beyond, out on the flat lands, night lying cold in shadows still.

The way through the woods that dawn was for him the crossing of a place of fear. There the wind broke bounding upon the dimmed slopes and chill; wings shaped before him, dull forms went by sleight away and all about was the grim attendance of the dark. Evil of intent lay in stealth everywhere, it seemed; was creeping even within his very roots so that he had but his courage and belief of trust to stiffen him in his going.

Light came sluggishly into the day. Theuda, rising from the cheerless reaches of the forest, found the Scaur still quietened at the close of night. Dogs gave their greeting to him, their tongues burning at the rawness of his hands. Later, they left off and stood merely looking about; or settled again to their dozing. For Theuda was held, trapped in himself and beyond moving.

'Theuda!'

It was Uhtred first then Eudo who came out. Others were called and fires struck up: there was all the welcome of a homecoming in it. Yet Theuda could not make words to his friends. Smiles touched limply at his face and he would grasp each man's arm in the fashion of greeting; but there was no answering in him.

A passage of days followed without change. Witu, with his youth and his willingness, would have spirited Theuda up with quipping and laughter; and Fer, dogged in his ways, made trials of talking him from his silences. But there was no means for this: Theuda was apart with his grieving. And beyond the grief of loss, he saw also the turning of his dream, the tower of hope torn down; so that now his pain, his rancour, had workings of fear and confusion within. No more could he hold to anything, no more the emboldening against hardships of the way. All was gone.

He looked instead for strength in thoughts of Ead's death, sitting long alone up on the rocks working his sword's edge with the stone. At other times he went, as if to the hunt, and kept watch along the river, there for his chance. But never did Ead come, never did he see the tall woman with the sow's head that Romac had spoken of.

Back at the Scaur, he would find Deor by the evening fire, and Corm close to him, turning much with smiles and blandishments in his voice. To Theuda, Deor would always give his greeting and call him forward to the fire; but even there, harboured from the rise of night, Theuda would sink away into himself and be lost.

There was an evening when of a sudden Corm spoke up to Theuda across the flames.

'Why does Theuda not share his sorrow with us, his friends?' he said. And pressing on into the silence: 'Perhaps he thinks it too great a thing for our lesser minds?'

A scornful gesture of dismissal was Theuda's only reply.

But Corm, with a burning meanness now in his face, spoke on, even past Deor's restraining touch.

'Then let him hear me! I judge his tireless show of grief a thing of ridicule. He grieves and for what? A woman! Pah! I say he finds glory in it all, that it is no more than a preening. Such a thing is not worthy of the Scaur!'

Leudi's arm was there but too slowly: Theuda had sprung. The lick of flame at the brand end made shapes a handspan from Corm's face. And Theuda's anger hardened into words:

> *Chill black*
> *The night;*
> *Grim full*
> *Its passing.*
> *Ill spews*
> *The mouth*
> *In falsehood*
> *Of friendship.*

Yet the taunting was not without some good. For the next day, with the sunrise, Theuda went again to the hunt. He put the riverland behind and went far away into the forest, the dog making bounds of excitement ringwise about him. Sunlight hazed warmly and a looseness of breezes was on the drift in the branches. Everywhere among the birds of the forest there was ceaseless exuberance.

And so, after the heaviness of his days, Theuda took courage and came once more to know all of a hunter's joy. Early on, down in a chasm's shadowing, he made a kill with the spear; and then, with a surge of eagerness for the light, he took to the open grounds of the woods on the heights, there to give trial of fortune to his bow.

Through the passing of that Hazelmonth day, Theuda ranged the forest lands in strength. At noon, by a startling bright well-head of the slopes, he made offerings of his hunt to the god and vowed himself risen again in belief. It was far on in the day, just as the sun fell away to the hills, that he came again to the Scaur and all were in wonder not only at

77

the achievement of his skills but also at the changed seeming of his bearing.

'There! Look!'

'Where?'

'Up by the rocks. Beyond the beech. Two of them.'

The words, hushed with them squatting in the ferns, died into silence. Kuno and Theuda were boulders of stillness. Birds flew; a sounder of swine trooped off downwind.

Later, they went to the rocks.

'There!' said Kuno. 'It is as I said.'

And indeed, by the rocks, where the earth was soft black, the print of feet lay puddled together.

Their gaze went slowly about to the forest. Awe of puzzlement filled them; disquiet at what was not right. They stood and distant flutings tranced them in the windlessness. The twilight of hanging storm was sleeping beneath the trees.

'Beohrt saw three this morning. By the falls.'

Kuno nodded.

'Now they are seen every day.'

'But what can they want, Kuno?'

'Nobody can say.'

Their voices crept cautiously beneath the silence. And then, in their pausing, there rose in them a rootless dread, a sense of dark spirit; and their skins roughened with it. Together then they took to the trail and made back in haste through the deadened forest.

For days now the women had been appearing in the forest close up by the Scaur. Both singly and in groups, they would stand and stare though never did they speak. And among them were often to be seen the naked, dark-ringed bellies of the bearing women.

At the Scaur, a gathering was waiting about the fire. At the news, there was quiet clamouring on all sides.

'They will say nothing of what they are about,' cried Fer. 'I called to one but she was still and would not speak. When I went to hold her, she ran from me.'

'Witu and I met up with some on the cliffs above,' said Brun. 'It is shameful!'

'Tell them! Warn them off! Who do they think they are?'

Deor brought his control on the tangle of voices. But to his asking if anyone knew of the women's purpose in coming so near to the Scaur, nobody gave answer. When lastly Deor's eyes came to Corm, Corm's face opened up.

'Me?' he said. 'Should I then be the one to know such things?'

'Corm, the Scaur calls only for the truth of things.'

'But I know nothing of the women and their designs. By the god, I swear this!'

The clenching of forces overhead had tightened. Night darkness was gathering into the afternoon and the air had so thickened that skin was now glaireously damp. The forest too had set into a massiveness of quiet where shadow went densening by moment and branchwork stood as stone.

Crushed and low, the sky hung down upon the land through to the day's end. Distance had the growth of storm sounds in it, boomed trundlings moving out among the hills. Briefly and again, rain came touching and was gone. Always night seemed forestalled.

In the Scaur, no ease was to be found. The men stood about, braced to a readiness, and their faces turned always to the sky. Speaking was scarce and with voices kept flat: it was a spirit time of power.

It was later, by the last of stern deadlight, as the shattering volleyed with speed and silver upon the hills, that the storm rain came. Spaced and heavy, dropping in egg bursts, it doubled then and grew thickened into downpourings that settled to steadiness.

'Romac!' called Theuda from the tallow-bright darkness.

Across the rodding fall of the rain, the fleshman came swiftly to the hut. He shook himself dogwise and looked at Theuda. The tallow caught urgency in his face.

'What then, Romac?'

'It is not good,' replied Romac. His pointed face wrinkled

rain from it. 'Not good at all.' The storm put its noises
between them. 'Today, this very afternoon, he vouched himself. Before all of us. About the women.'

'Corm? So?'

'Just now – I saw him. He was down at the split pine with
three of them: the one they call Ead and two others. They
were talking.'

Thoughts held them silent. Then:

'They saw you?'

'Yes. I was not looking on a need for stealth.'

Again the rain made a drum of the hut.

'Perhaps it was nothing, Romac,' said Theuda.

The fleshman looked at him and then at nothing.

'Perhaps,' he replied.

The bright flickerfloods and the battering overhead passed
away soon enough to the flatlands and beyond. But on across
the breadth of the night the storming falls of rain held firm
and the darkness was massed with the sound. Late, as if cut,
it broke off, then redoubled but again soon fell away completely. Dripping was left in resonance; and slowly gleaming
of day crept into the sky.

Shouts were in Theuda's dreaming and were there as he
awoke. Sharp dazzle of sun staggered him in the doorway:
wetness held light everywhere. The shouts were moving
down into the forest. By the gateway, Kuno and Acur were
with Uhtred.

'The others have gone on,' said Kuno as he turned. 'Uhtred
will stay. You had best be with us.'

'But what is it? What is up?'

'Romac,' replied Kuno even as they went. 'Something has
happened to him.'

Water filled the forest. Spoutings ran everywhere, earth
gave sucking, sun glinterings dropped cool from each leaf.
Down at the stream, the riot race had both jaggings and
sinuous lengths in it, mud and cream scum and kick-ups
against the protrusion of rocks. Higher, at the falls, the noise
of it put them to silence.

Three days – of sun and bright rain flustered by winds – three days the Men of Scaur were in the search, returning by half-light dampened down in heart: for no track nor trace had they found of Romac the fleshman.

'But why?' they said. 'How can it be? He who knows so well the ways of the ground and of the beasts too. How can he have come by harm?'

And:

'Why then, by night and by storm?'

So they hoped and willed themselves to it; but then, by sunfall on that third day, of a sudden it went from them and they took themselves to sorrowing, Beohrt and Fer most utterly for they the fleshmen had long run the trails together – but the others sorely too, for all of friendship and from the dread of an unknown death.

Till then, Theuda had held from speaking. But when it was all done and only sadness was left to him and to the Men of Scaur, he went straight to Corm.

'Corm, you are known.'

Eyes cold with mockery turned on him.

'What nonsense is this that fills you now, Theuda?'

'You are known and yet will not speak. Have I to say this to the Scaur?'

'Say as you will. You can show nothing. They will think you mad. Everyone knows that wordspeakers have power and madness together. I shall laugh.'

'Romac came to me, Corm. Late that night. He spoke of you and the women, down by the split pine. You will not laugh.'

Corm held to silence for a moment.

'Then Romac spoke madness too,' he said. 'I have no knowledge of this story. And you can show nothing for it, I tell you.'

The sun had gone to the hills behind them. An air of chill in shade was about.

'So what did you do with him then?' said Theuda and now he was without guile for he was driven by sourness of balking.

And to this Corm went rising into anger.

'Be warned, Theuda! So may you gibe with words – but I tell you: a day comes when you will eat dirt before me. And then too I shall laugh!' And now his anger drew in so that his eyes chilled over and the words of his speaking came spattering cold:

'And you can take your threatening elsewhere! It brings no fear to me – only scorn. And remember – I have a knowledge of you too. For was it not you who spoke last with Romac? Did you yourself not say this? Perhaps I in my turn am to say this to the Scaur. What then for you, I ask?' And he spat a hawking on the ground.

No further talking was between them.

It was this exchange with Corm that, in those days of the summer's passing, was to bring Theuda often in thought back to Cynric; and, in this, there was no peace for him for still he could but know the death a wrongful one. And he knew too that from this thing of shame was more: for the strife of feud that lay between Corm and himself was but a harvest fruit of this dark death. Thus was the strife merely a furthering of pain for Theuda in his overcast memory of the river girl and the dream.

The month went through to its end. During all this time, there were women in the forest about the Scaur; and now movements of them, pale and formless, were even to be spied there by night. Watchword shouts were made to them but never to any avail and gradually it began to be that this silent presence became as an unearthly spiriting to the Men of Scaur. Soon they found themselves shuddering to pass by as they went to the hunt. It was one of the men who said:

'It is worst with the barebellies. Even if you were to go as if to touch them, they would not move. They know too well how the bearing womb gives awe.'

Though they saw so much of the women, of Romac there was no sign. And so it had to be that the Scaur sought its strength of number again by one sent up.

None of the hiddenness of way that had brought in doubting on Acur did he have, the new one. Ease of manner was his and laughter too: there were chub cheeks creased about a budding of mouth. His body had weight and was not gainly; yet, over this, lightness of spirit gave grace. His name, he told, was Bobba.

When some – Beohrt and Fer with Theuda – saw him alone and put the question to him, amusement replied in his eyes.

'Women?' he said. 'Here in the Scaur? Would you allow for it?'

'Some would have it so. Would you be with them?'

'Not I! A madness!' And his face laughed out again.

And so Bobba came to the Scaur.

It was in the first days of the Vinemonth that Ansi came to Theuda.

'Deor bids you to meet with him along the north ridge by the noon sun. So speaks the Tineman.'

Gladdening held Theuda as he climbed. For the past while, deadness of spirit had lain within him and the sleeping of his nights brought only messed dreams where neither end nor sign of purpose came in. Now, as he strode below buzzards of the wind, he carried a berry growth of hope inside him.

High by boulderfall above the forest edge they met, there where warmth of sun lay fast within the rocks and stilling airs gave peace and all the surety of enclosure. There beneath the open sky they sat alone and felt come into them the forces of the place. At last it was Deor who spoke:

'Theuda,' he began and now his words came following heavily, 'you must know that in these days the Scaur stands set about by menacings and doubt. Outside, in the forest, the women wait yet do not speak; within, our differences have set us one against the other and so brought us new uncertainty. It is true, as Tineman I can guide and only guide: force has never been of the Tineman's power. Yet I must tell you of the sadness I feel when I know my time passing from me and see so little strength of peace among my friends. I lead – and shall lead – as I can. But to you, Theuda, I would speak of what comes after me.'

It was later, after they had left the place and walked the hills in the long measures of their talking, that the moment came to Deor for him to make his bidding to Theuda. Ranked forms of wind were there high up by the peak stone of the ridge; and grasses, coarse grown, lay bent beneath among the rocks. Words gusted, their bodies were tugged: yet rightness was in the place for here openness of earth and sky came touching together.

Sun flames brightened in his hair as he turned to Theuda by the stone and in his face was formed the gravity of his love.

'Now, in the god's name,' he said, 'and by all the truth of friendship, I ask of you, Theuda, son of Aldith, that you stand for me as companion, as Tineman's counsel and strength, till the winter feast; and that as such you make with me the journey to the sacred ground on the day of Idho. So do I call you as tanist.'

With both hands, Theuda grasped Deor's arm and his face shone.

'To you and to the god himself, Deor, I give thanks! Gladly, with all my heart, gladly will I stand as tanist to you.'

And with that, there high on the ridge, the two embraced and the wind was surging about them.

Down by the forest bounds, Deor paused.

'Before his day is come,' he said, 'the Tineman is charged to relate to his tanist something remembered from long ago. None has ever known quite what or why it is – only that its telling is a way of old and may not be lost.

'It is, as it were, a memory of a distant people where the men were ruled outright by women. They had the power, the women, and used it well. It was they who shaped the law, who controlled the trade and gave the teaching to the young. It was they who even taught the men the skills of weaponry – and though by this they gave the men a strength, still they held safe the power by keeping them from all holiness of rite. The women alone made the holy

84

sacrifice: indeed a special death was ruled for any man who stood as witness to their secretness of worship.'

Immense lay the forest lands below and the sky stretching was an enfoldment of all. So winds passed with birds borne high, dark fleet of shape across the fist of light; and they, the two alone, they stood far out in the wildernesses of thought and words were as gone from them. At last, shivered by a touch of fear, it was Theuda who spoke:

'But can this ever have really been? Surely it is just some curious dream recalled.'

Deor smiled and shook his head.

'Who can say? All I know is that things once happened are never forgotten – it is as if their very happening makes them part of us for ever more.'

'But Deor, it could never come again. Never!'

'Perhaps this is why the story must continue to be told.'

It was on the day following that Theuda, falling asleep in a secret corner of the wood, was visited afresh by his dream. As before, she was there and stood but partly seen, fair of head and supplely smooth in limb; and Theuda knew himself called as ever by a need for service to her. In his dreaming, it seemed that he cried out to her, once that she should show herself to him; and then again to her unmoving, even as he awoke:

'Aithne!'

And suddenly there was the day once more and resin warmth and leaf and birds of the bough and, through the wood, the tattling of jays. And amid it all was Theuda, his heart punching and his head hanging dazed by the dream.

He pressed his hands' heels to his eyes and searched to find the dream again. Then he sprang and said aloud to himself in anger:

'She is no more!' And knocked a tree with his head.

But no such ease of rebuttal was to hold. For again and recurringly so, the dream came into him in those broadening nights of the Vinemonth, darkly and foreboding for sure yet still engendering new trust of belief, bright and strong. Now he no longer woke with the river girl's name but lay silent in the dark, struggling with happiness.

When Deor brought Theuda to the Men of Scaur with pronouncements of his tanistry, ovation and all the uproar of rejoicing had carried on through the day. That night, by the blaze, the men were called on to give the greeting; and to this, each had come before Theuda and spoken the words. After the others, came Corm following and gave due honour; but later he held off from any further shows of joy. When, next morning, he went from the Scaur and was absent for a space of days, no great heed was given; for the disappointment in him was known to all.

It was in the season of Eadha, when the nights had grown to the measure of the days, that he returned. He said nothing of where he had been nor did anyone question him for now he seemed well in spirits and prepared to take his proper place. Among the men, most said that he had gone from the Scaur to seek a purging of himself. A few however were less sure.

When first he returned, he made directly to Theuda and was smiling.

'There was no gain in enmity between us. Let it be of the past.' And he put his cheek to Theuda's.

At the new moon, they held the feast to mark the closing of the summer's days. In the lower reaches of the forest where the trees grew great and pillared, ivy climbed in profusion. This had been gathered and many of the bees that loitered in it as well; and from the two, ale of substance had been made. Vatted, it was carried to the inner forest, to a place beneath brave snoutings of rock where a bowl form lay tucked on the slope of grass. Fire was lit and the night was to be passed with ale and laughter in the encouragement of mockery of the dark days to come. It was to be a taunting of fear.

Late, when the moon's thin shred swung high over the cliffs, Theuda walked from the flamelit gaming and out to the forest margin. There he paused, looking long into the tree-dark with bursting eyes; then stepped out and was gone.

Sightless, he felt a way down among the trunks. Mast and twigs crunched here; then beddings of leaf and of plush moss inlaid with stone. Branches knocked and snagged at him while over above, owl bands were on the move. When water guggled at his feet, he slid and floundered in it; but then came quickly clear across.

He stood in a strip of land under stars. The noise of the feasting was far and lost. He was apart.

He began to make pacings that quartered the ground; and, as his eyes grew to the starlight's dim, trotting came to him too. Later, he stopped abruptly from this and was searching about in the night. When he went off once more, it was now with a vigour of urgency so that he was hurrying from his halting again and again as if maddened.

Loose rollings were in his eyes and he let his neck back into an arch. His body was hard pumped and with it he strained against the night, forced snufflings blowing in his nose. Turf broke soft to muddied coolness as his feet raked; and then, bending in a rage of thwartedness, he was down, driving with his might headfirst among bramble and reed. He rooted in and further; then tore by bucking. His neck swung and twisted and hauled up; and with it, his chest was resounding with dull groans. Beneath him, small skids of mud opened and between his fingers rose an ooze of slurry.

Later, the thrashing quietened in him and he stood up. For a while he waited there, gulping, and then walked back into the forest. But when he came in sight of the feasting again, he stayed hidden and was fighting with himself. From there, he watched them at the fire where now they were leaping the flames in laughter and calling on the god with a wildness.

Passing of water sounded in the dark nearby and a voice spoke:

'Does the tanist keep himself from us then?'

And with that a shape of shadow grew into Acur. His eyes, pricked by the distant firelight, came in close.

'But Theuda, you have hurt yourself!'

For a moment still, Theuda could make no words. Then, chokingly:

'I . . . the god . . .' he stumbled.

'The god?' The response was keen.

'Yes,' breathed Theuda, 'the god visited me.'

Helping him clean away the mud and slime of blood, Acur bent forward and whispered words into Theuda's ear. By the fire, shouts fountained up into the night and fell away again. Theuda's eyes were round and unseeing. He was shaking his head slowly.

'No,' he said. 'I tell you – it was the god.'

When Theuda was back with the others, ale-glazed looks fell askance on him for the firelight showed him roughly cut about and still wandering in himself. And now he sat alone and would not speak, turning merely empty eyes on those who came to ask.

It was only later, in the deeping of the night, that what was locked off in him came free. It was as they trailed home by brandlight, strung out with voices leadened down by sleep, that Deor came on Theuda resting and Kuno with him, giving support.

'He is weak,' said Kuno to Deor.

'I tread the earth,' intoned Theuda. 'I . . . I . . .'

'Come, you are tired,' said Deor.

'Remember!' said Theuda suddenly and urgently, pushing his hand away.

Together, the two men went to lift him. But he was swinging his head, with groans, and a force shook in him. And then, with a sudden fury of belief:

'Remember her!'

The shout, enormous in its power, tore open the night. Deor and Kuno stepped back. Out ahead, the voices had been crushed to nothing. In the backwash after the cry, a little wind appeared turning among the trees.

'She is strong,' muttered Theuda. And now his head hung on his chest. 'So strong!'

8

And then, of a sudden, among the midmost days of the
Ivymonth, the forest was on fire. Mere sparkings had come
first, randomly in the green, and were as nothing. But they
lay banked up in their multitudes and smouldered so that
finally kindlings happened and everywhere scatters of flame
burst out. Above the forest tracks, canopies of furnacing
spread across the pale sky. Further in, on the slopes, the
firefall tiered down in towering, brazen flanks and engulfed
all below.

There came too a greath wealth of mists that rose out of
each night to lie as clouds upon the land by dawn. Diffusions
of light, vast and pearly, grew with the sun; but later, with its
falling, there was a thickening once more and the last of the
day went dragged down into a ruddy brash. With all this, the
earth steamed and smoked, dampness and warmth together,
and it was a time of fruits and much gathering.

As the days made on, the bite of rawness crept in. Dust of
rime appeared coating the ground and the tips of fern
growths went curling to sear. And now, as the year fell to
frost, the forest lands sounded with the angered groans of the
buck in his rut, and everywhere the wooden smacking of
antlers crossed. The Men of Scaur heard it with brightened
eyes for the god's show of power in this season was always a
thing of awe to them. They made offerings at the fire, of
blood and the juice of seeding, and then went down to the
riverland under the hazes of noon, treading lightly, stealthy
with lust.

As tanist, Theuda had shown himself forceful in vigour
and a bringer of steadying control to the Scaur. Yet, in his
hidden self, there was much disquietening. For what had
happened at Eadha had set him about with seclusions within

and of these there was no speaking. Deor saw it and urged him to free himself; but for Theuda each time the words went failing from him. At length, however, there was a day when Deor threw down his bowl with an oath.

'Then, by the god, do as you think fit!'

And he stalked from the hut.

But in those days of the rut when all the noise of the god's power was about in the forest, the trammels tightened into a fierce straining in Theuda. The sound of the bucks' troating, concealed but angry in the folds of the fire leaf, brought him to testiness and feelings of muzzled force.

On one such day, he too went to the riverland, making his way down through the echoing woods, dry of mouth and pulsed up. There, in a damp thicket out of sight of the sky, he found a girl idling, fox-haired with breasts apple-tight, whom he took with violence across the moss bark of a fallen tree.

'You are angry,' she said afterwards, turning green eyes edged with mockery on him.

He left her and roamed far, seeking assuagement of what still lay taut in him. Upriver, along the alder banks, he stopped. High in the woods, bucks were about, with noises of warning and then the rattle cracking of antlerwork. He held still, ear-bent, and felt with his listening a tumult of agitation beginning to bloom in him. Then shudders came and he went as if spun, thrown loosed upon a sapling growth nearby. He struck and hauled at it and all its limber power fought back at him, with bending and bowing, and the trunk, slimy beneath his body, tore into him so that he had gouts of blood mixed with the wood juice and mire.

And then suddenly, in his tussling, he had taken to boring and ripping up and it was another buck against him, firmly holding and then thrusting back whenever he should happen to give; and his neck rocked and stampings were in both his arms and his haunches. He made deep snorts to voice the fight in him; and then, twisting, he saw them standing by. With the fox-haired one were several others and all were gape-faced as they saw what was in him.

His arms swung and his feet were scraping. When he went, his boundings at them brought cries and scattering but the voice was winded from one of them as she fell beneath him. As she went backwards, the ring marks showed strongly on the white bulge of her belly.

He trampled into her and the power of him made air come in sullen pumpfuls from her mouth. He dropped down and went butting at her with his head while knee-blows and fists milled against her. She was bloodied now and loose as if sleeping but his teeth making hungered snatches at her belly drew her up howling and she rolled from him. He was gathering himself to spring again when a massive hoofing struck at the straddle of his legs and as he doubled, a sodden bough shattered on his head.

His eyes opened to sky. Immediately, swollen sickening of pain brought his knees up and, with it, wincing closed off his face again. Blood drivelled from his temple and in his head there was a boom of stunning. Somewhere too, there were voices and busyness. He sank back into a night of collapse; but straightaway, it seemed, ropes were gnaw-tight at his wrists and his hands were being tugged from his balls. The ropes twisted him so that he went with his mouth into the grass and a foot stamping on his head gave him mud to taste. When a further rope held him by the neck, he was brought to standing and drawn off into the woods.

After his staggering, a voice was close to him:

'Ead will have her own way of thanking you for this.'

The ropes on his arms pulled him stretched as they tethered him to trees. When they had fastened him taut, he heard their words harsh and businesslike about him for a while. Then they ran off, leaving just two who bore cudgels.

He was down at the shoulders, head slung low. Where the foot had caught him, pain flourished steadily till he felt himself completely swallowed by it. He retched quietly and spoke of it in groans. Through blood mattings of hair, his eyes peered aslant at his guards. Smiles of malice were their answer; and a slow fondling of clubs.

'She will break you,' said one.

'But not too quickly,' added the other.

And they laughed.

Later, the coarse rant of rooks burst out overhead and sunlight came in a gash through the cloud. Theuda's head rolled back and he sucked hope from the new brightness.

A short whistle upped into the air.

'Bobba!'

The fat man stood above, hands hooked on his belt, and was grinning.

'Let him be now!' he called down with good nature to the women. 'He is to come back with me.'

But they answered with shouts of abuse and raised angry weapons at his approach.

'Now, now!' said Bobba, pausing. 'Let there be no fight in this. He is a friend of mine.'

But still his laughing ways were nothing to them. Together, of a sudden, they ran at him and killing was in their manner.

Bobba's hands whipped and sunbright stars flashed from them.

'Come!' said Bobba as he cut Theuda down. 'We should be quick.'

The women lay with their moans on the leaves, making clutches in blood at the stars' work.

Up into the fastness of deep wood they went, Bobba leading. Once, they heard outcry of shouts back below and, peering, caught sight of the troop of women. One stood apart, looking up towards them. She was tall and wore a white sow's head.

'Ead!' said Theuda.

Near to the Scaur, he turned to his companion.

'I would thank you, Bobba. I think my life was not to be mine for much longer.'

Bobba's eyes glittered in the roundness of his face.

'Chance took me to you, Theuda. The rest was only a friend's deed.'

Theuda touched him in greeting.

'You throw well,' he laughed.

'The stars give me joy of skill, it is true,' answered Bobba.

From here into the Reedmonth, with its low swiftness of sky and its bustling leaf-squalls, all lay quiet in the Scaur though outside in the forest, the silent presence still gave unease. The men went as always to the hunt but now with the days of the year going ever further into their decline, they kept much to the Scaur and to the great hut there, where fires would burn throughout the length of the coming cold and its nights. For now they stood but fifty days from the winter feast and thus it was time for each man to draw back into the measured thought of things. And now, more so than all, Deor and Theuda were often together – for they were needful of a clearness, an encompassment of what was to come about for them at Idho.

A day came that was all but still night. Heavy canopies of cloud lay soaking above the land and everywhere there were massed depths of coldness and weighty saturation. Below the Scaur, the forest stood deadened, spiked blackness and the darker blemishes of the evergreens.

Deor struck the post with force unleashed.

'By the god, the madness of pride in you!'

Theuda swung his head low and would not speak.

'Then let it be as you will!' said Deor, barking. 'I can do no more!' And, fire-faced, he turned from him.

'But Deor, it is not so,' said Theuda. 'Only that I am so set about by fear of things I cannot know. You must have trust of this: there is no speaking of it in me.'

Deor swung back and there was striking in his eyes.

'You have said this since Eadha! And you go on saying it – even now after this other thing with the barebelly. By the god, Theuda, what is becoming of you? This mournfulness, this closing off! Have you forgotten? You took the oath. You stand as tanist to me. Soon the Scaur will have great need of you.'

And now Theuda himself was sparked. So that he made answer in words of bitterness:

'Don't tell me of my duty to the Men of Scaur! I know it well and shall see it to its end with joy! This I swear!'

'You say this – but hear me yet: I tell you that what lies locked in you may come to such a strength that finally it brings unmanning of your power.'

At this, Theuda fell back into dejection of thought. But Deor, now driven loose, had no stopping of himself.

'And Eadha?' he said and his face was close before Theuda's. 'And this other thing? What of them? You say nothing to us! Nothing! Yet you would have us believe in some so-called coming of the god!'

'He came, I say!' shouted Theuda. 'By his very name, I swear he came to me!'

'And how,' thrust back Deor, 'how are we to be sure of this? How, I ask? What would you have me say to Acur who repeats to all that men of madness have said as much? For all I know perhaps he is right. You slept that night by . . .'

'That spirit night by the stone, you mean,' said Theuda and now with calm.

But Deor could not give him answer. His head was shaking.

'Well,' said Theuda, 'if a madness has its hold of me then so it must be. It is true, I speak words, words that come to me from I know not where. Perhaps that is a madness. Yet even so, Deor, even in what you may call my madness, I can only say to you the truth: the god came into me.'

Sombre glooming stood about them in the hut. The fire had lapsed to the frailest winks of embered heat. Outside, drizzle falls now further veiled the latening sky.

Deor worked his fervour on the fire. Wood cracked sundering and new flames were kicked from out of ashen glow till robustness flared again. Then to Theuda disconsolate he turned once more and spoke his words, now heavy with sorrow:

'Dread fills me that we should have come to speak in such a way. I had no mind for other than to be of help to you in these days of darkness. This you know.' His speech was softly held for grip of will now toiled with the blaze within.

Theuda nodded to this.

'Deor, I had such need of your belief and trust,' he said. 'That you of all should hold me in doubt was what brought me to dismay. I was alone.'

'I tried,' replied Deor. 'For many days I tried. You gave no help.'

'Deor, I had no way!'

'You! You had no way!' Deor's voice had swollen up again. 'Then how was I, ignorant of all, unguided, to hope of finding one for you?'

'It is true,' said Theuda and suddenly it was as if the fight had gone from him.

'You asked for help then closed me off from giving it!' Deor cried. 'Me, Deor, your friend to death, you spurned!'

'I did not mean it so. It never seemed like that to me.'

'You did not look! So trapped in thoughts of yourself you were!'

'Yet I would share all of everything with you. This you know. But in this there was no way of sharing.'

'Did you try? Did you?'

'Yes, I tried.'

'No, Theuda, no! Not once!'

Into the growth of flooding dusk, dissension bloomed vile between the two. Sullenness and loathing of the quarrel held Theuda apart; while Deor, so unopposed, went ever further outside himself in the surging of his assault. When, with the coming of night, the Men of Scaur returned, it was to find the Tineman and his tanist wordless and separate with the pillaring flames between.

Days passed on, with all the expanse of now greater nights, and the fault remained. Despondency lay about the Scaur as a stench and among the others bewilderment went unanswered for neither Deor nor Theuda would speak of the matter. It was Kuno at last who took courage and faced the Tineman.

'I know you as a man prouder than most,' he said. 'Yet Theuda, who loves you as himself, has greater pride for fear is in him and he dare not speak.'

To this Deor gave no answer. Yet Kuno's words lay working in him and, soon after, he went out in search of Theuda.

The meeting of the friends anew was a thing of wonder. It came about on a day of breathless cold, when raw branches stood as thronging cracks upon a paleness of sky. Fast among the open vaultwork of the lower forest they met, near to where it gave over into the spaces of the riverland woods. There below a bank deep and bronzed with leaves, Deor found his tanist. Light fell flashing on his hair and trailed plumes of his breathing rose white across his shoulder as he bent to the gutting of a beast of the hunt. When he looked up from his task and saw Deor, then for a while both of them stayed as they stood and the sounds were only of bird mob and the distanced drumming of falls.

Later they made fire and roasted flesh of the kill; and through the passage of that day they talked, quietened and with all the silences of friendship. When at last they kicked the fire down and made back for the heights, there was laughter of ease growing in them. Just below the entrance-way, in the crush of dead light, Deor stopped.

'Theuda,' he said, 'we have fought with the bitterness that comes only to the strife of truest friends. Of this, there can be no forgetting. Yet now, with your companionship refound, I shall turn again to the approach of my day with joy in my heart.'

And Theuda, half-formed in the shadowlight, reached out to touch him and answered:

'For this, Deor, I truly give thanks. There is some way in which this fight was clearly meant to be for it has brought to us understanding and greater strength.'

That night, the forest lay firmed under frost. In the Scaur, bowls were raised and the faces flamed with rejoicing.

As Theuda went alone in the forest one day soon after, the bushes before him opened and a group of women appeared, standing across his path.

'Ead would speak with you,' said one of them and it was a command.

Theuda shifted the spear in his hand and glanced gap-wards to his side.

'No,' she said tartly, 'there is no need. The talking is to be peaceable.'

The clearing where they left him was a place grim in spirit feeling. The sky of wind seemed lost in far-off heights: only raw stillness was there and the leaf mess underfoot was cold and lightly fetid. After he had waited a good while, he was for leaving; but in that very moment there came from behind a boomed proclamation of voice:

'They say you are mad.'

He twisted round. Nothing was there.

'Ha!' he shouted at the forest.

'That you have ideas of the godhead,' said the voice.

Theuda spat angrily.

'Who says this?' he called back. 'What do the women of the holm know of me to say this?'

'Not the women,' said the voice. 'The Men of Scaur.'

Theuda stared at the leaves.

'Some of them say that you are falling demented from notions of glory, that you would rival the god himself.'

'Where are you? Show yourself!'

Deadness continued to lie around for another while.

'There are things to be settled between us,' said the voice of a sudden, vast and somewhere near or far. 'You hurt one of mine. She dropped the child. It died.'

'And Aithne?' bellowed Theuda. 'If you are speaking of hurt, what of her?'

'The girl knew the law. She hurt herself.'

Theuda groaned. But the voice came immediately again, now fiercely:

'They say it was your madness made you attack. Well, I warn you – next time I shall kill you! But these things shall be of the past.' The voice had suddenly changed. 'We shall speak instead of the Scaur.'

Theuda stood numbly waiting, giddied still by the brunt of memory.

'Soon you will stand in rule there. We, the women of the holm, would seek an understanding with you.'

And Theuda, now gathered in himself, spoke back as tanist:

'May there always be understanding between us. Truly, we would wish it just as you.'

A bark of laughter rebounded at him.

'You? You wish understanding with us? All the Men of Scaur have ever wished from us is pleasure and subservience. And it is this that we shall no longer have: we seek a sharing with the men. As a sign of trust, we ask first that you let us have entrance to the Scaur.'

Theuda snorted.

'The Scaur has always been a place for the men alone,' he said.

'This can change.'

'No!' And then: 'Besides, we follow a different god. In this, there could be no understanding between us.'

'Yet might not a joining of belief bring greater strength? Your god and Alphito, the wise one – together they . . .'

'No! It is you who speak madness. We are separate, the men and the women, quite separate! We look for different things.'

'And what of Ura then? When the god joins with Alphito?'

'That is different.'

The voice waited, as if settling itself; then spoke with a measured pace:

'Could it not be that completeness comes to all only with the joining of halves?'

High scud opened then and power of sun fell dazzling down upon the wooded slope and so was gone again.

Theuda blinked.

'You are mad,' he muttered to himself.

Later, when the voice was there no more, he went in

among the trees. There was nobody. But by a fire-struck oak, he found a scattering of white bristled hair.

'Let the others be,' she said quietly. 'You are yourself. And remember – if the god wants you, he will take you.'

Pucks and twistings of wind were in the white downpour. They shaped in the flake fall then vanished with hushed buffetings into the trees. Occasional birds, enormously black and heavy of wing, steered past and away: otherwise there was only the massive slowness of the fall and the building of deeper quiet. Out over the river, the whitened plain stretched up into the sky.

Below ground, in Dillo's lair, the hiss of damp wood held steady.

Lit under by the fire, Theuda's face was blank and weighted as her voice hung in the air about him. He slid a glance at her but her eyes, well-deep and dark, were not seeing him. Her speaking too was from elsewhere.

'Should I then do nothing?' said Theuda. 'When he comes into me, I cannot know myself any longer. Then I fear for what I may bring about.'

'And what could you hope to do, Theuda? We think ourselves able to put our control on things yet surely this is but a dream of pride. For in truth we are always led; and what leads is already within us. To follow with trust is our only need.'

'But Dillo, I must know! I am soon to be Tineman in the Scaur!'

Cross-legged she sat and now was rocking; and by her silence let the surge in him sink. Then:

'Still you call for it,' she said. 'Still you hound yourself with this will to know.'

'But a Tineman who does not know – what kind of leader is that?'

And she rocked, now slow and in her rhythms. A quivering of her eyes beneath their lids troubled her and her voice emptied into depths.

'A true leader, Theuda. I tell you – through doubting comes wisdom which is not knowledge. But it is true – to trust in this is to walk hidden by clouds.'

'And a man who takes this way? Where does he end?'

'Truly it is the walking that gives joy.'

Four of the year's long months had passed since last Theuda had met with Dillo and now as the cloaking stole lightly over the land above, he spoke to her of all the things of his heart. Of his dream and its return he told her; and of his quarrel with Deor the Tineman.

'The pain of this still lies deep in you,' she said. 'You have not mourned enough the loss of what was before.'

'Mourn?' he replied and seemed to scorn her words. 'How should I have mourned? And anyway,' he added, 'now all is mended.'

She nodded. But later, when the day had gone, she stacked the fire and used oils of the woodlands on his body. And it was then, in the cradling of pleasure, that tears surprised him.

From here across the Eldermonth and on towards the winter feast, Deor and Theuda strode out much together.

The snow went and though the nights were reaching to their greatest span, the days became dry and light. In the pinched isolations of this season, all hard feelings among the Men of Scaur were put away and bonds grew swiftly in strength: it was a time of companionship. Gladness held them all and ever more so to see the Tineman and his tanist now foremost in this trusting of belief.

And then, in the last dwindlings of the year, shifts came into the sky. Two days before Idho, the night unfolded with winds streaming out of the north, the bearers of new snow. Gritted falls of it swept about in the flarelight at the hut and long into the darkness, stormings bayed booming down from the heights.

Sun burst light everywhere in the stillness of dawn. Now polished clear, the sky stood tautened out overhead, rigidly cold. A fox, far out, sounded at hand; and from below, passing along the cliff, ravens' dark crunking rose hugely. All about, blue shadow held ice.

In the Scaur itself, the men readied themselves. The winter hunt, on the eve of Idho, when bodies were furthest from the plenties of summer, was for them a feast of hope.

Feet stamped and voices called sharply in greeting, with urgency and laughter together in their expectations of joy. They took arms then and, with their dogs, went from the Scaur down into the frozen forest. Division of grouping was given though for now they trooped together: later they would go their ways for the drawing of the deer.

On the forest floor below, snow lay in evenness underfoot. But as they made up higher again, into the grounds of the storm winds of the night, they came on spines of rock and earth blown clear into protrusion and, all about, steep drifts massed up. Dogs arched bounding through with prickles of glinter thrown up in mists and then, in pursuit, the men broke their ways, waist-deep. Beyond, they were out on to slopes under sheltering with all the hope of finding deer.

And indeed, soon after, a gasp of grim awe arose. For high on a mound beyond a dip, an apple tree grew, hooked and knobbed with age; and by it, in all the splendour of its palmed head, a white buck stood, proud and pranced up on guard.

Nobody moved but each eye was now turned on Theuda.

'Take him!' breathed Eudo. 'He is yours!'

'You must!' added Fer, from behind him. 'It is the only way this ill can be taken from your future.'

'Ill?'

'A white buck by an apple tree on the winter hunt is of bad boding for the tanist.'

Theuda eased an arrow from his cocker and drew it on the string to his jaw. As he sighted the head against the buck then there crossed in him a thought of his life to come. Tremblings ran upon his bow arm, wildness stirred in his head and the loose was uncertain. The arrow went fair but flirted away to drive hard into the trunk. The buck gave his snort and sprang off. Then a groan hung among the men.

Deor came forward and spoke calmingly.

'Theuda is one who has walked clear of fate before now,' he reminded them. 'We can trust that he will do so again.'

From there they went variously, spreading wide to make a line of tightening about the deer. With Theuda were Witu and Brun: it was for them to go furthest and hold the southern edge. They crossed a dense corner of the forest and then moved apart, each with his dog, to take up station.

Theuda was below a bluff. He watched Witu and Brun go fading among the brake and then settled himself. The dog stood close beside him.

Up on the rim of distant cliffs, winds ran and streamed out featherings. The sky was blue; the sun steady and low. The forest around was emptied of movement.

Somewhere above him, a stick cracked. He looked up and staggered as the sky roared and darkened from him.

Later, he found darkness still and sour earth stuffed against his face. Then a hand was touching him and he rolled to bright day.

'Bobba, what happened?'

The eyes over him had surprise in them.

'I . . . I heard the noise and came, Theuda. The cliff top must have fallen. I pulled you free. Are you hurt?'

Theuda sat up.

'The dog?'

Bobba looked down and shook his head.

'He was a good friend,' said Theuda and his shoulders sank in his desolation. And then: 'Once again you have come as help to me, Bobba. A man has need of friends like you.'

'E – oh – e!'

Deor's far cry bounded up off cliff and spur. With this, the line was to be under way.

Noon sun cutting aslant on the cliffs saw the deer turning back and about at the foot. Dogs held them so while on a ridge above, the men stood ranged with their bows. Arrows flocked whispering down on the silent air: no man could bring himself to utterance in this, a moment of such reverence. The shots carried with all the trueness of the men's longing and marks were found over and again. From stumbling, forelegs crumpled and the weight of head and muscled haunch swung bodies over to the ground where each would lie dozing to its death. Then, with the dogs called off, the ring was opened for the does with fawn at foot to run clear.

At last, all movement ceased. The Tineman gestured his tanist to him and together they went down from the ridge. Now, as by custom of old, Deor bled each beast with a cut to the throat and when the last was done, he turned the bloodied knife on high to the Men of Scaur.

Exultation rang up in shouts against the cliff: jostling echoes brought it further to tumult. And so they came running from the ridge.

Now too they laughed and song burst from them as they worked their knives that slit and strove. Blood came bubbling thick and richly dark, grey bulge of paunch rose out with bland and snaked-up mass of bowel, smooth lay dark liver close by tallow fat and lung. About them as they made the cuts, the dogs prowled and watched; while above by far into the blue, spans of wing kept eyes of keenness on the work in hand. There was joy and beauty everywhere.

At last they rested and gave the dogs their due.

It was later, as they bent themselves homewards to the Scaur, that Kuno spoke in secret to Theuda.

'I went back,' he said. 'To where your dog had died. I found the place and climbed above.'

'I was blessed with luck, it seems,' said Theuda.

But Kuno shook his head.

'Who held the stations north of you?' he asked.

'Why, there was Bobba who saved me. With him were Corm and Acur. But how is this a part of it?'

'There were footprints in the snow up there. Theuda, I think the cliff was meant to fall on you.'

With the last of low forgelight in the sky, banks of cloud came in from west of north. The covering brought murk and, in the murk, new snow in steady falls, dense and ever fattening on the ground.

Now, against the force of greatening night, the doorway was closed and comradeship bound about the Men of Scaur. Darkness and cold stood locked in might around: the year lay weak and hopes were frail.

Some of them went at first light.

Hush again was in the air and fiery chill. The snow spread deep in tracts and in the forest, boughs and brake were weighted down to sag. As they climbed, the men looked out upon a land overlain and shackled tight.

This was the day of Idho.

Leudi and Ansi stayed. They, the Tineman's men, barred fast the door and brought forward Deor and his tanist to the new-awakened fire. Water, earth and flame they gave to them for cleansing and then the drink appointed by the rite.

Now by the festal, springing fire, the two sat alone. No words could bring them further in their search of trust: this final, utter strength they could only seek within the unspoken trusting of their bond.

It was with the midwinter sun standing proud of summits to the south that the door fell open; and into the fields of unclouded light the Tineman and his tanist came forth. Now wearing the skin and the might of horn, Deor led with Leudi and Ansi there beside him. And in the twofold place behind strode Theuda, blind and beyond himself in his belief.

Upwards from the Scaur they went, along the tracks of those gone before. High ahead, smoke climbed above the trees and the sky was burnished out and cold.

At the winter ground itself, close to the upper limits of the forest, they found the Men of Scaur rowdying and urgent. Blood of the hunt had been tasted and now, with their chests streaked and caked, they moved around the fire, swollen up in laughter and angry expectation. About the ground were placed the heads of bucks; and before each tongue-bitten mouth stood a bowl of the beast's own flesh well-cooked.

As noon came, the Men of Scaur ringed the ground and the calls in chant began. Within and facing, stood the Tineman and his tanist who, as the power arising, now wore the pricket head. As uproar beat upon the air, the tanist put himself in stances of attack; then gradually came edging in. But with the men's cries now gathered up to howls, none heard the buck groans working in the tanist's chest. Only when he began to move on at the trot did their rabble roaring teeter then fall away to puzzlement and mutters of alarm.

The troating now groaned and stormed in the tanist as he stood with shoulders hunched before the Tineman. The men came closing in but suddenly were running for the pricket head had thrust down and slashed.

They howled and beat at him as they dragged him from the fallen body. When slowly the Tineman rose to his feet again, oozes of blood were messed on his ribs.

Chaos of noise was battering about and harsh cries crowded at the tanist's ear. Now eyes that had turned back towards the Tineman saw him raise a hand of calming and assent. At this, the chant picked quickly up again.

Behind the masks, Tineman and tanist were now faced and still. Then the Tineman stood forward a pace and made the gesture of demand, with arms outstretched and straddled legs. The roaring returned and doubled force. Into the tanist's waiting hand a helve was pressed and he was loosed.

Immediately, the Tineman went down, two men holding him by the antler palms. Above him, brightness went flashing high across the open sky; then fell coldly, swift and sure.

The two assisting bore away the antlered part. The others, chanting again, now gathered in to partake of the flowing force.

Later, when all was burned, they left the ground. But as they passed back down the mountain way, a multitude of crows appeared, wheeling columned up upon the air, dark and voiceless. At this, the men dropped their heads and hurried on, mouthing words of power to cover them on this now most dangerous of days. For till dawn when Ailm, the day of birth, would come, they must live unruled and threatened by the overcasting of the spirit dark.

At the Scaur, they burst ice from off the pool and washed away the passing of the year. Then, calling in the dogs, they sought harbourage within the hut. No fire would burn there that night.

Outside, the moon had already taken stand above the lustre of the hills. Below the Scaur, an owl was shrieking and everywhere new flourishings of frost were tightening down in grip.

9

'Theuda!'
And again:
'Theuda!'
And:
'Theuda!' they cried.

Above them, layered mists of birch twig banked up sharp and purple; and, from out of this, the scabskin rock rose starkly cold. High upon it, he stood alone.

The salutations broke about him and low sunlight shattered into dizziness in his head. He stood arched towards the appearance of day, face flung back as the growth of light brought him new birth. Moment by moment, its rise crept down on him, from crown first to chest and frame; and all this time he was shimmering, as if fire of life was in him as never before.

So his rule came to grow with the sun. And when at last the brilliance covered him fully, the voices sprang to a great rush of joy. Only then did his eyes open from the closed-off burning of his wonder. He strode down from the rock and smiled broadly to his comrades now ringed about.

'It is come!' they said to each other. 'The day of Ailm is truly come!' And they turned to him with planished faces.

And then they were laughing and clasping each other as their relief broke out. The icy darknesses of the dead year had borne hard on them; but now the ranging of light was refound and, with it, the knowledge that the new force was alive amongst them, that the dread ascendancy of night must begin to fail before the power of their belief.

With the next day, the Birchmonth came in and Theuda proceeded into the glory of his life. Strength flowered in him and a certainty too – as if he had never known doubtings nor despair. Clarity held firm in his thoughts and the ease of his ways carried itself to the Men of Scaur so that now differences and any edging for praise or preferment were as nothing and forgotten: happiness was rife. By night, while they slept, Theuda would sit by the fire and the flush from smoulder and small, sprigging flame would illumine the contained might of his joy.

The new man came up and was received.

'I am Gort,' he said and had taut limbs wherein there was a toughness as of vines. He was even of mood and, from the first, put himself with the fleshmen, Beohrt and Fer. And they, soon coming to accept him, took it upon themselves to bring him into all the gathered secrets of the trail. So again the fleshmen's group was whole and this was considered good by all.

Gort had not been long in the Scaur when he came to Theuda alone. It was of a morning as cloud shapes slowly marked the land and a light edge of wind flickered on the snow. Theuda he found at the doorway, dressing the blade of a spear.

'There is something I would ask of you,' he said. 'Something I do not understand. About the Scaur.'

Theuda looked at him and smiled.

'The women,' said Gort and Theuda sharpened. 'Who is their man here?'

Theuda put down the spear.

'Their man? In what way would you mean?'

Gort gave a shrug.

'I do not know. Just that I had understood it so, that there was one who was here for them.'

It had been late that summer, he said, when the women came upriver to put in their say for the choosing of the next man for the Scaur. Gort had known too well how matters stood and so had spoken in such a way as to please them.

'I was to be one of the Men of Scaur,' he said to Theuda. 'This I had decided long ago. It mattered little to me if I should have to pretend some allegiance to the women of the holm in order to be chosen.'

'So they think you are for them then?'

'Quite so,' he grinned. 'They told me that I was to act as might be; that their man up here would speak to me when the moment was right. That was all.' And he shrugged, pulling a face of contempt.

And now Theuda spoke back keenly.

'Then, Gort, you must see how you stand with crucial power in the safeguarding of us all,' he said. 'When he shows himself . . .'

'I promise you,' interrupted Gort, 'he shall be made known. I swore this long ago by all that is holy.'

As Gort was going, Theuda held him back.

'Did they then speak of the man as already in the Scaur?' he asked.

But here Gort had no sure answer. So Theuda gave him thanks and bound him over to secrecy.

In the days that followed on, Theuda held himself stealthy in vigilance; and, in this, it came about that his scrutiny fell most upon Corm and Acur. Corm, as before, lay always just beyond his trust; and it seemed too that Acur's eye was often darkly poised on him as if in assessment. Once, he observed the two together, fast in speech below the drifts of the outer gateway by falling day.

Unease of this brought troubling to him; yet in spite of it, the Birchmonth days hung lulled in the aftermath of the winter feast. With the forest lands muffled and bedded under, none travelled far – though once some of them made a sally out in search of bear and came back, ruddied up and spark-eyed, with stories of the mountain snows. Of the women, there was no sign. Everywhere, all was quiet and still.

Late in the month, Eudo came to Kuno.

'Is all well with him?'

'Why do you ask?'

'I have seen him by night, Kuno. Several times. Once he was speaking words into the fire.'

'It means nothing. These are things wordspeakers do,' said

Kuno. 'No, I would say he stands well enough and strong.'

To this, Eudo answered slowly nodding.

'It is true – he gives his strength to all of us.' He stood as lost a while and let the anvil lie smooth beneath his hand. Then: 'Yet, Kuno, within he has some other thing. It is a gnawing of sorts. I do not know what.'

Small winter birds went clouding by and flocked together on the ground.

'You mean at Eadha?' asked Kuno. 'And the winter feast?'

'Yes. It was as if . . . as if the god had come too close to him. But not just then, Kuno – always it is near, this thing, always! It is as if he wants it so.'

'He wants it?'

Darkening came to Eudo's face.

'His dreams of the god are full of the joy that brings danger.'

'But what should then be done?'

'We can but watch and stand by him,' replied Eudo from his darkenedness. But then he touched Kuno and assurance was in his hand.

'He will keep strength,' he said. 'Do not worry – all will be well.'

But only days from then, early in the Rowanmonth, it was already otherwise.

Covering had come by night into the sky with softness of winds; and rain, with drip and drizzle, had begun to pock and carve out the banks of snow. From there, the winds gathered, pushing in heavier falls of rain, and then withdrew, leaving the forest under calm but snagged by trails of mist, with snow now grimed over and thinned to streaks.

Kuno made a party with Theuda and Witu; Brun with Corm and Acur another. Down from the Scaur by noon they went and dogs were with them for they had boar in mind that day. Soon spread out, they began to set a line about the quarters where in winter the sounders often lay.

Stealing over sodden slopes went Kuno and his group. They came upon no freshly trailed marks of boar; but, later, shrilling rose and shouts went up from south that brought them running to the place. There they found the others, standing gladsome by their kill.

'And Theuda?' said Acur and looked about with eyebrows raised. 'Where is he?'

None knew; so Kuno, leaving them, went back to trace the way in search.

It was by a bank, steep with grass, that Kuno found the Tineman. He called his name but Theuda, standing turned away and leaning on the slope, gave no heed to him. Then Kuno, coming closer by, spoke to him again and now more softly in a growth of fear. Theuda slowly turned his head.

Voidness was sleeping startled in his face. The chewing of his jaw went idly round and grasses, matted pale, hung sprouting from his mouth. Drowsing distances were in his eyes: Kuno knew himself but dimly seen.

The head went down again and tore up further tufts in laze of unconcern yet intent with deepest hungering. The mouth went on. All about, the forest stood in dampened chill.

'Kuno! Kuno!'

Acur's throated voice was near below. Kuno sprang round and reached the edge.

'Here!' he cried above. 'Here! All is well!' But his words came tightened, oversharp.

Corm and Acur looked up at him with curious quizzing.

'And Theuda?'

'I found him. We shall go back to the Scaur and meet you there.'

'We shall come with you,' they replied and began to climb.

Kuno, aghast, ran back and pulled Theuda up from his grazing.

'Quick!' he hushed into his ear. 'They are coming!'

But still the eyes looked back at him from far removes.

'Theuda!' he shouted quietly. 'By the god, I beg of you! You are the Tineman!' And then was striking him about the head with cuffing blows, light and fast.

Now Theuda's face went cockled up and surprise of

waking made his bite of grasses drop away.

'What?' and 'Where?' he began in mumbling tones; and then, with that, he let himself be drawn to running, led by Kuno to the cover of the trees.

Panting crouched, they saw the other pair come up, stop paused and then go swiftly passing on.

For a while yet, Kuno stayed with his head bowed in the steaming of his breath. But then, with the clammy quiet settled down once more, he drew himself up.

'We should go back,' he said. 'They will miss us.'

Theuda's face was still awry. Without sight, he looked away into the forest: words were still far from him.

'It happens often then?' asked Kuno at last and now he spoke with gentle words.

Theuda's brow tautened up.

Kuno laid a hand on his arm.

'Theuda,' he said, 'your love of the god has brought you close to him. And this is a thing of marvelling to all of us. But you are still the Tineman and we have need of you. Take care, I beg of you, that this love of yours does not burn the very soundness from your mind.'

At this, Theuda turned and the desolation of vision lay immeasurable in his eyes.

'It is not in my power,' he replied. 'Truly it is not in my power.'

'Then shall we, your friends, be of help to you.'

'Help? And how would you think to stave off the god in the force of his designs? It was he who called me, many months ago before I came here though I did not know it then. Now I can but follow with strength and heart.'

'But, Theuda, the Scaur!'

'What the god gives me, I give to the Scaur. Is that not enough? It is all I can do.'

But to this, Kuno answered in the quiet speech of truth, saying:

'No. No, Theuda, it is not enough. We of the Scaur need you not only as Tineman in spirit but, for the vigour of our

112

being, also as a Tineman seen to be the Tineman. When you are visited by the god, we are bereft and so weakened. This cannot be.'

Theuda looked long at Kuno.

'It is true,' he said. 'This cannot be. The Scaur is all.'

'Without the Scaur, there is no Tineman.'

Silence and raw air surrounded them as they made their way back to the Scaur.

That night as he sat with the others, Theuda was driven to speak to them of the Horn Fellow and the life spent in the pursuit of honour. Power and fervour came into his words and the faces about him shone with elation to hear him so. Above the crack and putter of the fire, his voice rose and fell resounding and a spirit of dream held them all. At last, his words were emptied from him and he was left fallen into an exhaustion on the edge of blackness.

They all came about him then and gave thanks with the warmth of their hearts.

'All my life I have searched for words of what it is,' said one of them and it was Uhtred, 'and now you have found them for me.'

And from afar, with closed eyes, Theuda answered:

> The man will laugh
> And bend his bow
> Though another
> Will surely guide
> The shaft in its falling.
> To venture all
> In the god's name
> Must be the way of men.

Winds of weight streamed out of open skies off the ranges to the east. The mess and matter of the thaw had gone clamped under new frost; and now, backed by the wind, everything was locked in with ice.

Chink-eyed and cloaked about the face, Theuda headed

down across the gale, securing himself by branch and rock as the glassed ground made to escape from his feet. Harrowed by the blast, tears of cold squeezed free on to his cheek. Dimly, through the watering, he saw the meadows rinked and dazzling beyond the turbid life of the river below him.

He came now of his own accord. For only days after his words with Kuno, it had happened again. Under the first of starlight, he had come to himself alone in the forest. For a while, from his waking, the raptness had still lain softly in him; but then grim horror had brought out shudders as he saw around him the grass ripped and torn. Earlier, the sun had stood high as he left the Scaur; but of the passage of time from then he had known nothing. And so, in his fear, he had brought vows on himself, that he would seek wisdom from Dillo of the Bank.

The wind tore flutings and running veinwork on the surface of the river; in the creeks, bedded reeds, sheathed bright, pronged up from misty ice skin. Neither beast nor fowl was about: it was a time for truce and holing up.

He was flash-blind as he came down into the lair but from the darkness she spoke his name and, with this, a calm spread over him. Then, with his eyes opening up, he saw her seated beyond the fire. Hunkered on her lap, a large hare was sucking her nipple.

'I have been waiting for you,' she said.

'I nee yo hel, Yillo.' His mouth, stunned by the cold, would not work.

She brought him close to the fire. As they sat and listened to the wind, she was easing peace back to the hare with strokes of her hand. Her eyes were wide; her head, newly shaven, was a shell merely hazed with stubble. She watched the fire and was waiting.

Later, he was speaking of his life. It was not to her he was speaking – her presence was for him as an ear of the darkness around in which he thought to see his truer self. Of his calling to the Scaur, he said:

'For those many months, I believed the one of my

dreaming to be her I was to serve. In Aithne, it seemed she lived.' He shook his head, unbelieving. 'Now I must think that there was in her some disguise, that her death was meant to show me this. So now I follow the god and he possesses me in fullness. Yet still the dream comes into me and I no longer find understanding of it.'

And from the darkness apart came the words:

'The god alone rules you, Theuda. You see no other.'

'But the god calls! I must follow!'

'You have come here and spoken of fears yet will not listen,' answered the darkness. 'If you want to follow the god and be a leader of strength for the Scaur then take heed! Follow him and honour him, for sure – but do not exclude all else, at your peril!'

'What else?'

A silence came in.

'I can only warn.' And then: 'Ask Deor – you have great love for him.'

A hare scream broke out in the dimness and warmth of fur touched against Theuda in its passing by for freedom.

Theuda staggered under the barrages of wind and light on the slopes. He ducked and twisted with his head to throw off the giddying and, beyond his will, his teeth chattered busily. Yet there was speed of determination in his going and no regard for relenting when he fell.

Eastwards he went, into the mouth of the ice wind, crabbing round the edge of hills; then upwards over wildernesses of crackling grass and slab slides of snow towards the peak that stood alone.

Higher, on the mountain backs, the wind rose pellet storms against him and burst his cloak into snap billowing; but still he made on, tucking down and angling himself aslant, towards the tusk of black rock standing above him against the emptiness of thundering sky.

The gash up was floored with ice. He slithered on its steepness and could not advance. Above, below the tusk, the opening was dark and edged with frozen fangs. He put himself back in the gash, wedged on leg and shoulder, then swung the hand axe up into the ice. He hauled on it then braced and swung again. Steel streams poured down on him as he rested. Then up another arm's reach and again, slowly.

Frenzies of the gale awaited him at the top. He stood grappling with it in its shrieking spate and then tottered his way towards the opening. As he bent himself into the unknown dark, icicles tinkled clattering about him.

Inside the peak, the storm was somewhere else. Brightness of day bounced in but beyond it fell away to murk. The cold in the place was fearsome.

Theuda's whole body was filled with shakings and his mouth had dried out. He peered in search of what he had come for yet did not want to see; but there was only rock and the cloudings of his breath. He fought against his body but the shaking would not succumb. At last, however, he swallowed and eased his throat.

'Deor!' he croaked. 'Deor, it is I, Theuda!' And then again, breathed: 'Deor!'

The storm strove on outside with enormity.

Theuda's nails tore at his cloak. His eyes swung and all of his fear was yammering in his pulses.

'Deor!' he shouted.

Booming sounded far down and a faceful of chill air puffed from out of the unseen. He sank back and so it was that a glisten happened high up.

With fists iron-hard, he stepped towards it.

On a ledge was Deor's head, tanned dull by smoke and with sleeping eyes.

'Deor! O, by the god, Deor!' He sank to his knee; then steadied himself within and spoke with more evenness: 'Deor, friend of friends, I come seeking counsel of you. You alone can know; you alone can speak truths for me.'

Deor looked back stolidly. There was rime on his lips.

'The god is taking me,' continued Theuda. 'He is taking me and this gives all the strength of joy. Yet so too does it keep me from fullness as Tineman. It is because of this that I am here. For I fear it may bring the Scaur into weakness. Deor, where is my way from this?'

Exhaustion of despair was in Theuda's voice and he hung now agonized in wait. But expectation passed on with silence to further waiting and from there gradually into failure of belief.

His head sunk low to his knee.

In that very moment, the great wind's sound began to fall away from him. The blast streamed on but now it was as if it blew in some far-off place. With this, a cavernous peace came in and warmth mantled over him so that he thought himself brought to the safety of sleeping hearths. Freedom had gone from him: he could only crouch bent and stripped of will. Yet now intense gladness stood bright within him for suddenly perceptions of glory were at hand. His eyes closed; an awesome power rose above him. And, greeted, he went forth from himself into the heart of darkness.

SUNLIGHT SHINES I TREAD THE EARTH STRENGTH IS BEAUTY SEED IS HOPE HONOUR ME REJOICE

DARKNESS DREAMS I REST REMEMBER HER SHE IS PALE SHE IS COLD SHE IS STRONG SHE TOO IS OF YOU

Outside the hut, Ansi said to Theuda:

'They had words yesterday. Corm belittled Kuno's bravery and Kuno laughed and said that this could be put to trial whenever he chose. Bobba was there too.'

Frost fire hung raking in the windless air. Away in the east, first light was growing. Overhead, the sky was pitch blue and starred.

'Earlier, just as the moon was setting, I woke and saw them leaving,' added Brun. 'Kuno told me that Corm had called him out to make pursuit of the wolves. It was to be hand weapons and one dog only between them. This way it was to be a proving.'

'Madness!' said Theuda grimly.

Bobba joined them and swiftly the four went down from the

117

Scaur into shadowed and deeper cold; and so turned north on tracks that rose towards those distant parts of the forest which lay up beneath the greatest peaks. Loping took them on steadily through the murder chill of sheltered places and then slowly up to where the now lofted sun was striking among the trees.

There, they broke pace and made deliberation for the search. Theuda quickly set them in their quarters and himself took dogs along the eastern edge.

It was in the scrags of the upper trees, on a ridge towered over by an ice-hung castling of rock, that he heard it. A roistering of snarls burst rising to him out of the still and sent him high-stepping fast, down through the tangle of growth. Vantaged on an outcrop, he saw below Kuno and a dog alone fast embroiled with a small pack of wolves.

This within the blinking of an eye. Then:

'Kuno!' he shouted and was out in the air plummeting.

He struck down and went arse-high over on the leaf mass and bush of the ramp. Knock-blown and dazed yet he found his feet again and ran in with all the speed of attack.

Strength is Beauty! now burst again in his head with such a sense of love and kinship that he was empowered beyond himself. One wolf turning took his flying kick and went staggered back; another was put to pause by a fist blow of crushing weight. And immediately, Theuda was in by Kuno together.

And even as the wolves gathered themselves to strength again so did Theuda's dogs come round; and then too the group from out of the forest. Shortly, two wolves lay pierced and still and the others had gone their way with haste.

Kuno, in his gasps, laid a hand on Theuda.

'Thank you,' he said, wiping blood away. 'I had come to think myself taken in the god's design.'

But Theuda, still in the anger of attack, replied sharply:

'Where, by the god, is Corm?'

'He went round west from here. We had thought to find the wolves further in.'

Eventually they came up with Corm. He was slow with hobbling.

'Kuno!' he said and stopped in some surprise.

And when they told him what had happened:

'Well, I heard the noise of the fight,' he said, 'and was coming with all speed. But there must have been dark ice. I fell and think I was perhaps senseless a while.'

'Well anyway, I was in luck,' said Kuno. 'Theuda came to lend a hand. And before that, the dog had held them fearlessly. You were right, Corm – he is the dog to take for wolves.'

'He . . . the dog was all right?' stumbled Corm.

'Yes. You chose him for us. Remember?'

'Yes, of course,' replied Corm quickly. 'I was forgetting.'

'Good fellow!' said Bobba, turning away to pat the dog.

And so the matter was left to lie. But later that day, it came to light again.

'Kuno!' said Theuda, whispering his words by the midnight fire. 'I beg of you, be on your guard! I believe the hunt today was all in ruse.'

Within days of this, the Rowanmonth went out and that of the Ash came in.

10

The year paced on. The sun's reach grew and, with it, slack airs came to ease away the clasp of winter cold. Succession of flaws burst on the forest with drives of flattened rain but then were gone: for now predominance of light was there. Everywhere the nose of bud braved out.

In those changeful days, Theuda went often to the riverland and sat with Dillo for her understanding of the way of things brought steadiness to his ever growing joy of belief. When she spoke, it was almost as if her voice came from within himself, as if she were in some way now part of him.

Once, he said something of this to her. She remained in her stillness a while. Then:

'People who are alone have a great bond, Theuda.'

'Alone? But how am I alone?'

But to this she made no reply.

In the Scaur, the Ashmonth proceeded in good cheer, bright with the sounds of preparation for the coming spring. Stain scabs of dampness were worked off forgings of iron; newly laid-up strings fitted to the sturdy, skin-backed bows; bracers were tried; spears ash-shafted and heavy nets were each thrown for balance – all the work of the short days was put in readiness for the hunt. And with this came the reawakening of spirit, the yearly leap of heart as they saw the trusting of belief bringing in triumph over old, frozen fear.

So too did rejoicing rise in Theuda. All about, he saw only strength and wonder; and in himself the sureness that his course was true. And so it was that an exalting followed him through his days.

By night, the dream was now with him again. But ease had come from Deor's words: no longer was the fair one whose face he never saw of torment to him. When he made mention of the dream to Dillo, she would still answer hiddenly, speaking of this unknown one as if she were just a figuring of some other thing. But to this Theuda could only shake his head and stare beastlike into the fire.

It was in those wayward, failing days of winter that the men began coming in with news of the women being back in the forest about. And with their return came new consternation; for while the barebellies were the same as ever, cool-faced and unmoving, the other women were quite changed in manner. Now there were smiles flaunted with drifts of whisper and laughter and much enticement by eye and glimpse given of shape; and the men, kept from such things through the months of snow, rose fervently and made on to approach. But each time they were luckless; for the women, still laughing, would fall back, always beyond reach. Never once did any of the men get to couple and in this there was much disgruntling and sourness for them.

And then, quite as suddenly, the women withdrew. For a while, the men paused, sensing some trickery. But later they went out to the forest and then further to the woodlands, casting about though with their hopes hedged by misgiving. And indeed there was nothing, no sign of the women. Even on the holm, there was a seeming silence: only stillness and smoke flagging lazily above the trees.

But the grudge and rankling which this left behind was soon drawn out into clearness. One afternoon, dogs breaking into voice down by the gateway brought the men running, there to find but a girl child standing alone. They asked her her purpose; at which she opened flower-blue eyes on them and spoke her words chant-fashion, each falling as sharp as a drop of rain:

'I am bidden so am I bidden to tell that no pairing shall be no pairing at all with Alphito's women unless up here they say yes up here in the Scaur!'

Her high tones rang into the nothingness. And so she would have sung it again but quickly Theuda came forward and sent her on her way with his answer:

'Tell friend Ead that such a thing is beyond thinking.'

For several days the child passed up and down through the forest, humming and playing her games as she went. And with her was borne the parrying of words. But then one day she was there in the mist with her eyes and her chanting of a new message: that until change was made, the food sent up was to cease.

This was met by a gabble of outrage for here was seen to be the undoing of trust. When they had cried: 'So shame on them!' and 'No, not this! They cannot! Food is sacred!', somebody called out that the threat was easily answered – let them know that equally no more flesh of the hunt would be sent down. At this, the men gave a growling of satisfaction. But Theuda shook his head.

'To counter thus would be merely to open a trading in spite,' he said. 'Remember, the god grants us food and his favour may not be wasted. I say the flesh shall go to the holm as always. Let the women play with the keeping of faith if they will.'

And so the child was sent away and did not come again. And immediately, the milk and bread, the meal and cheese were no more. But urged by the Tineman, the Men of Scaur turned from this and went often to honour the god in the hunt; and, among themselves, no further mention was made of the women and their shameless resort to reprisals.

Yet, with the coming passage of days, a breath of unrest began to move again in the Scaur. Theuda chose to ignore it; but then, by a buffeting, cloud-driven day falling towards the close of the month, it could no longer be so.

He put down the sleek weight of badger that he had just brought in and found the grouping of them there before him. Corm it was who stood forward and spoke:

'Theuda, I stand here for those of us who would have some agreement of reasoning with the women.'

'Ha! And how?' Theuda walked close up to Corm and looked him in the face. 'I would say ruttishness has put weakening in your head.'

'You may call it weakening,' retorted Corm, stung. 'We see it as sense. And it is not freedom of entrance that we would give them – just that they should come at our given word from time to time. We think that this might find acceptance with them and so end this foolishness.'

'Perhaps,' said Theuda. 'But it would not be long before they eased and turned your minds. Soon they would come, seemingly so at your command but in truth as often and when they willed.'

'But why? Why should they care to trick us so?' asked young Witu, his words wild in disbelief.

'Surely this is but a fancy of fear,' put in Brun beyond.

'It is for you to think as you will,' replied Theuda. 'But still I say to you that they have no place up here where all are given to the honouring of the god.'

'But what is it they would want?' broke in Witu again. 'What would they have from us by guile?'

'The power,' said Theuda, flat and firm. 'It is the power of rule they want.'

Crosscry of voice went up and in with slap of wind, indignation blooming over disbelief. And so they turned, sharpish in tongue:

'What?'

And:

'How possibly?'

And:

'Raving, stark raving!'

But Theuda faced into their words and was unmoved.

Again Corm was before him and speaking:

'We would have the matter taken to the count.'

There was all the blind look of determination in him, harsh in its fury of sureness. And still it showed in him, as a crazing almost, that night as the count was taken by the fire.

When the count however went against, he drew back. Theuda sprang up.

'So hear me, Men of Scaur!' he said. 'Twice has this thing come between us. Now let it be put out of your minds for good! I speak as Tineman and guardian of the holy strength and do pronounce it so.'

And with this, suddenly Corm was up and by his side.

'Friends!' he said and his eyes were pressing out of his head. 'Gladness of heart will have me speak and praise the Tineman who stands with us in such fervour of strength. He it is who leads us in the hunt so clear-sighted for the god and with all the power of will; he who speaks to right us in our ways, bringing us in safety from the deadfalls we could not see. By this, he commands us both in love and honouring of respect. With joy, I pledge myself to him anew: friendship and following may he always be sure of from me!'

Surprise held them all. But Theuda turned and, giving the touch, thanked him with due warmth.

It was only afterwards, under the cover of the ring of idling talk, that their glances came to meet so fleetingly across the fire.

It was on a night when stars pricked clear and silence, slunk curled among the forest trees, was everywhere about that Kuno said:

'Theuda, the Tineman is all. He must stand safe. He alone is our hope.'

And so they fell to quiet, there in the plenitude of night.

Long after, as clouds came across with a pittering of rain, Theuda put his question to Kuno. Even in the dark, Kuno's voice shone up brightened.

'Gladly, Theuda!' he said. 'With all of love and fortitude! May the god make strength in me for this!'

Before they went, Theuda spoke more darkly.

'Leudi and Ansi alone shall know of this, your tanistry. As witnesses. By secrecy of it, we may hope to draw Corm out. Now when he has openly sworn himself a friend, now do I think him most dangerous of all.'

The furze caught with cracking and Brun laughed. He flared another bit and watched the joining of them with thinned eyes. When he turned from it and saw the other three fires in answer far about on the hills, he threw back his head and stamped his feet.

It whipped up bright, the flaming, and he ran to other bushes, still laughing breathless with his delight, and fired them too. When the whole thicket line of old prickle was massed in light and noise, he ran off through the last of the early mist and made for the humpback of rock high above. He was laughing all the way and choking as his excitement tangled with the breathings of exertion. But he went without stopping for the spirit was in him and his legs gave tireless bounding.

From the rock, he looked out on the fires spaced around; and to the forest beyond where night still hung sleeping in the folds. But it was to the east that finally he turned and so kept his watch on the great ridge.

When at last the sun rim broke into sight, he faced back to the forest and shook clear his head. And now a happiness lay enormously within him.

Down below, by the furze fires and out on a rise in the trees, the others heard the horn in its echoing and rejoiced. For the Ashmonth had passed; and now, in the first of the Aldermonth, had come the feasting of Onn when the days once more were at measure with the nights.

All that day Theuda led the drinking and the laughter. New warmth was about under the shadow play of flocky clouds as if to sign the arrival of spring; and till the fall of evening the Men of Scaur were out and lazing by a fire. Bowls were raised and oaths of good fortune given to Leudi and Ansi for at cocklight they would set out and make their journey of hazard in search of one who, with the coming moon, would run free in the forest as the Sorel. So too were Uhtred and Eudo named as helpers for Witu the climber: he it was who later would go to the crags for the taking of the bird.

With the afternoon's end, clouds densened about the sun and Corm came treading softly to Theuda with an offering of ale. As he poured the ale, he spoke covertly:

'As a friend, I should warn you,' he said. 'There is one here who would harm you.'

Theuda drank and smiled.

'There is always one who would seek to bring the leader down,' he replied. 'It is the way of men.'

'But here in the Scaur, should it not be different? You know well how you are held in our esteem.'

'Not by all, it would seem!' laughed Theuda. 'But are you not going to tell me who he is, this one – that I may protect myself?'

Corm drank long. And when lastly he spoke, his words came swift and low together.

'I do not know him for sure as yet,' he said. 'And it would go hard against me if I were to accuse without certainty.' He drank again, golloping; and now, suddenly, a deranging grew in his words. 'But I tell you – I watch and, where others may pass blind, I perceive! You must know that I have seen how the shape of what is to come will be!' And his eyes bulged as he went from his speaking far into himself. Then: 'You have need of me, Theuda! I could be as a shield to you in these times of threat. Make me your protector! Make me tanist!'

The breathing beat of raven wing passed close overhead.

'Will you do it then? Will you announce it so?' he pursued. 'It would bring new strengthening to you. It would give joy to the men.'

'The ale is heavy, Corm. It makes your words for you.'

Corm held him with stone-dead eyes.

'It is a shame,' he said. 'I had thought you wiser. Then shall it rest with the god!'

'Truly, Corm, may all things rest with the god!'

Corm swilled down his drink and so went from Theuda, striding.

Kuno, who had watched, came up. But immediately the ease of air was broken by an upraised voice.

'Men of Scaur, hear me now!'

Corm was unsteady by the fire and was taking sucks from a bowl newly filled.

'Today we celebrate the coming of Onn. In these times of uncertainty, I feel it well reasoned to follow a way of old. For it is said that if, by the season of Onn, a tanist has not been put before the Men of Scaur, any of them may make proposition of it to the Scaur as a whole.'

Theuda looked at Kuno.

Kuno nodded.

'He has the right,' he said.

'Now when we are beleaguered by the women,' went on Corm, 'I say that he who comes in as tanist should be deft in his dealings with them. No other will do!'

Small shouts of agreement sounded.

'And with that in mind, I now put myself up for it. I can handle the women. With me, you will not want for anything.'

Straddled loosely and sagged morose in drink, he waited for the men's response. Fire pops came on the silence; winds of dusk were rising in the trees. All eyes went past Corm to the Tineman.

Theuda came forward and stopped in front of Corm.

'Maybe elsewhere in the law, it treats of such propositions made in drink,' he said with scorn. A shiver of laughter was knocked down as Theuda went on but now hugely:

'And I shall say to you that the Tineman chooses his tanist from among those of trust. And he shall have understanding with him and a belief in his holding of the power. This alone and before all: for therein lies the strength.' A slackening then came into him: 'My friends, I had thought to speak of this this very night by the fire. But now clearly it is to be told here. Kuno, son of Luned, is already asked. He it is who shall stand as tanist to me.'

Smoking hiss of steam plumed up as Corm emptied his bowl on to the fire. He held himself braced defiant a moment more; then turned and pushed a path through the crowding men.

This shameful act brought dismay to all. But then they quickly put it from themselves and came to Kuno with the greeting. To each, Kuno spoke the rightful words and beauty of gladness was alight in his face.

Now with the secret ascensions of the lark in its glory, the spring began to open out into skies bland and pure. Rain burst along with sun; and fresh winds came in following to shake the drops free. Already the first of colour was brightening on the forest floor, pricking up proud of the old growth.

As ever, wonder prevailed in the Scaur with this renewal. Yet, for all this, a certain spirit of darkening was about the place too and the men were drawn and sparky. There was the matter of the food; and moreover of the women themselves.

'Let's make a raid on the holm,' young Witu would say. 'There are bound to be lots of them longing to get tupped.'

And to this a rebuke would be given. No violence, no aggression towards the women was what had been ruled: time alone was to show them.

But in truth there was more to the men's unsettledness for they were weighted down by a break in their number.

For Corm had gone. To begin with, the men had simply said:

'He has gone to honour the god and make peace with himself.'

And:

'There was much bruising to his pride but after this he will be whole once more.'

And when he did not appear the following day:

'It happened before.'

And:

'It means nothing. He will be back when he is ready. He is merely assuring himself.'

But the days wore on, far into the month, and still he was not there. Then one noon, Eudo and Gort, passing down a cleft of the hills, glimpsed him, out in a wilderness of rockfall. They called greetings but he gave no answer; and when they made towards him, he ran off.

'There was something about him,' said Gort.

'It was his eyes,' said Eudo.

So things remained. When Leudi and Ansi came to the Scaur again in their success, it was the sign for Witu and his men to take nets and ropes and leave with the barred frame for the western cliffs.

In these days before the coming rites, Theuda went to the river and took leaf with Dillo. From among the remote distances, he heard himself speak of things that lay in disturbance within. Fears that he would not reach the achieving; that his own calling would end as a disorder to his rule; indeed that he was no Tineman of worth at all and was only leading the Men of Scaur with false promises . . .

After his speaking, he had felt the silence grow full again. And when later he heard Dillo's voice, he saw no movement of her lips.

'To make words of one's fears is all that is necessary,' she said. 'When it comes to it, you will simply do as you do. It is the considering of things that brings fear.'

Here in the enclosure of the bank, with the flood mass passing close unseen, Theuda came into a peace from himself.

The daubing had been done, long smears, bright-coloured for the blood and the sun, reaching out from the tawn to far on to the dark of wing. And so too, in the clearing above the plunge of trees, the bulked-up branches had been readied.

They went slowly and with their chanting that gave praise to the promised death. Behind the bars, the bird turned and battered at its imprisoning; and would have torn at the hitches below the thwarting-board to be free.

Four bore the weight. When they came to the clearing in the pines, they made the cage secure on the trunk posts and withdrew. Pegs were knocked out for the sides to fall away and, immediately, the eagle wings canopied over the breeze in search of safety and the sky.

Lined back, the men stood in their marvelling at the power

of spirit. All the while, the rap and pick of the hook beak on the board was breaking off into gusting and screams.

Later and of a sudden, they fell to a hush so that then, below the wind, there was left only the sounds of the pattern-bright bird and, in an opening of the darkest trees, the man. Stripped to a clout stained red, he stood silent and stern. At his side was strung the horn and, high above against the blackness of the green, he held a smoking stick of fire. He came forward to the bird on the pyre, slowly and with his body flickering with light cramps.

The bird paused at the man's approach, dropped its head and was suspicious of the wind-flaring flame.

When they heard him shout the words, each of the men made the cut and threw blood on to the pyre before running from the place.

Slowly the jolting calmed out of the man. Now close to the pyre, he turned and over him the wings opened vastly to mask off the sun. It was a moment when the spirit was greatly at risk but he knew what had to be and looked flinch-less up at the power of dark shape. Then he put fire to the four quarters of the pyre and went back to the trees.

Smoke rose in strength and, opened by the wind, showed the certainty of small kindling fronds.

Crouched on the cliff, their painted faces as flames in the sun, the Men of Scaur leaned out over the forest and listened to the horn in its violence. It soared out and came knocking back off the walls and steep pitches of the mountain ring beyond; and the wattling of it with itself put a span over all. There on the heights, with the greater tracts of the forest sunlit below them, the men were still and silent, held daft by the blocking of noise.

Theuda blinked and his eyes closed under the weight of light. Recall had him in the forest deeps of another spring, bound and beneath the angered horn. Again the mud was against his cheek and again the fear lying cold in his belly. But in the fear, the resolve bringing him back up to strength

and to a determination for his life and his dream. And so
when the horn stopped, he . . .

His eyes opened at the new quiet and found the expectation of all the faces on him. And with the happiness of
release, he roared:

'E – oh – e!'

And again, now standing:

'E – oh – e!'

The fringe of cliff exploded. Cries and whistlings volleyed
over Theuda's shout and massed out in the echoes of the air.
And then they had broken cover, the men, and now came
twist and streaming down the tracks, steeply in a trail of
flashed metal and their colours of gaud and so still with the
whoops and caterwauling. Below, birds of the forest flung
wildly away and went scattering high into the sun.

When, soon after, the men came off the cliff and entered
the roan coolness beneath the trees, all had gone back to the
watching quiet. They paired off and fanned away, whispered
calls of luck passed about as they parted. From now, they
would move as hunters with only a sound or whistle given on
occasion to tell of their positions. For somewhere ahead,
loosed into the breadth of the shining forest, ran the Sorel,
token of coming fortune for the Scaur.

The trees, stark as yet, stood striking overhead as the men
spread in from the cliff foot. For a while, Theuda saw the
pairs alongside. When next he looked, they were gone: Kuno
alone paced on with him. And now both were given over to
the hunt. They went bodies alert, slipping past cracking twig
and wand with rolling soft steps, sinews strung balanced
with weight of muscle. The land shape rose and they too with
it, now on rock, now easing up screefall to pass on to a height
where clear sunshine fell steadily.

Here on an edge, they paused and Kuno rounded his
hands and gave the boo-hu, boo-hu of the great owl. A
choughing answered from far beyond; and away east, from
the deep, the crossbill kipped in repetition. So Theuda signed
southwards and they went again, dropping down on to a

bank with bows held high and passing on into the closed thickness of pines.

It was well on in the forenoon as they went quartering a rake of birch that the jay call stopped them. 'Skaak!' it came and 'skaak!' and then faster and yet louder from down and way behind. And then it burst and became Eudo in voice:

'E – oh – e!'

Theuda and Kuno gathered themselves and moved silently in speed to where the dip of valley was to be seen. Over beyond, beech and oak grew great in force with bramble and mats of wintered leaf between. Sunlight, fostering the bud, lay there throughout and with stillness too.

They settled and let themselves be as growths in the brake. Eudo's cry came once more but still far back and after it the valley's quiet held firm. Bird pairs passed, small but furious fast together, driven by the urges of spring; and later, flicks of breeze appeared and skipped on by. And so with the forest, the two friends waited.

But suddenly beyond, movement was there. Sensed first then seen; and slowly too the shush of branchwork and scrub opening to be let slip. Their eyes tautened on it and, shortly after, they saw the dappled form emerge and stand swaying horn-heavy in the open light.

Whipstring of sound sent the iron leafhead hard from Theuda's bow. Fast and flat, but a wisp on the warm air, went the arrow and struck sweet. With a staggering, the Sorel was down and then still. Gayness of feathers grew neatly from its flank.

Hallowing and laughter of delight came from them as they made a bounding descent into the valley.

'The Scaur!' rang in Theuda's head.

'Truly, it was a Tineman's shot!' said Kuno excitedly.

There, curled soft on the leaves by the strength of oak, lay the Sorel and now merely with tremors and feeble shifts. Theuda came up with the joy of deed still soaring in him and had the dagger ready drawn when suddenly Kuno's hand touched him on the arm.

'Theuda!' he said and his face was pinched in puzzlement.

Doubt was rising fearfully in both of them as they approached. The Sorel stirred and Theuda, falling to his knees, was cutting fast to loose away the drawstring bonds. Kuno heard his groan of dread and weight.

'Dillo!'

Naked she lay within the pale skin, with eyes glossed large, locked open in surprise of coming death. Little puffs blew from her mouth; her tongue edged lightly on the dryness of her lips.

Now to Theuda's blurted words, her head shook slowly and she made as if trying a smile. Then she was shaping speech and quickly he bent to it.

'Remember!' she exhaled and the voice was scarcely there. 'Her, her too!'

But Theuda was struggling with his gullet.

'Who was it?' he said. 'Who did this to you?'

Her mouth ringed up again and her eyes were enormous with effort. She tried it but nothing came. Again and then suddenly:

'Corm!' The name came shot from the ring.

But here she caught on her speech and coughed; and so it was that her next word came vastly rich and fruitful with blood. Heavy and darkly frothed, it welled copious and went in guggling to spread out bibbed across her chest.

'Okokokokokoi! Okokokokokoi!'

In full throat, Kuno cried out the alarm again and yet again over the forest and heard it come answered up and redoubled. Then he turned and to Theuda still couching the body, fragile and stained, he gave his pledge.

'He shall be brought to it and soon,' he swore, gall-mouthed in his resolve. 'Till this is done, I put myself apart, outwith the Scaur!'

'Go then! It is right,' murmured Theuda out of his dazings. And whispered when he had gone: 'So be it by the god!'

It was late on in that fated day that, gathered silent in the Scaur, the men heard the dogs. Yelping of full flight came drably down upon the wind and made all as one rise in determination.

From out in the forest, they saw the dog troop chasing up towards a back of rock, high on which and clear against the weakening sky, showed Kuno fast springing with his bow.

Wordless, their spirit burnt out, the men placed themselves across the slope. Beneath the boldness of the festal stripes, their faces now showed grim, hard-jawed and dark with a need for what was about to be. They were held only by their anger and the shame.

Soon the bushes became busy with noise and then Corm was there before them in his stumbling flight. He drew up fast and would have turned his course but for the dogs now coming in. Havering held him balanced; but then he had seen the blindness of the men's resolve and was shuffling back to succour himself by the trunk of a blasted tree.

The dogs, arrived and called in under command, had fallen to loll-mouthed panting. Theuda walked up to the tree. Before him, Corm stood hunched and lowering. All the look of fight was in him yet and scorn showed sneering as he stared at Theuda through shags of hair. With a crack of a laugh, he jutted back his head and gobbed into the dirt.

From high above, the shout struck down. And, even within its sound, there came a breathing flight that punched iron into Corm as he turned. Two more such came quickly from Kuno's bow, both driven with the fierceness of loathing, and Corm's feet scrabbled as he fought against them. Then he was still and hung twisted fixed on the trunk, leering with hatred and in his pains.

Theuda drew near and looked at him without pity.

'You made this for yourself,' he said with words that were drawn cold-short from grief. 'Madness of envy has worked weakness in you, Corm. And you have put yourself beyond the love of the Scaur.'

Derision came in a snort from Corm. He peered out of a face clenched askew and spat again.

'So speaks the Tineman!' he mocked. 'And did he find his skill of words to celebrate the Sorel? Ha! They said she was a boon to you, that woman. Well, so too was Cynric such to me. So let it be – a death for a death!' And he laughed wildly and swung his head.

Theuda remained faced in stone.

'A death for a death!' he murmured. 'Truly, Corm, you have earned yours well.'

'Not yet!' answered Corm, now whispering coarsely. 'Not till you have heard me! You think it is me, that I am their man? That it was me who pushed the cliff on you? That when I go, you will be safe?' And laughter and the gloating of power gurgled in him. 'The women are nothing to me. I made use of them, it is true – but only against you. You are finished, Theuda! You will see. Even now the Scaur is lost! Even now she . . .'

Brightness streaking by Theuda's side ate into Corm's chest and was a star.

'Filth! He is mere filth!' spat Bobba, coming up. Then, seeing Theuda's outrage turn on him, he added with speed: 'Ask him then! Ask him about Ura! And who it was who told Ead of the girl in the cave!'

The sheerness of fury fell away from Theuda's face. He stared at Bobba, his lips opening uselessly.

Bobba gave him a confirming nod.

'Aithne!' came retched up in Theuda's groan.

Corm heard the name. His lip hooked briefly up, taunting, and a messed laugh choked in him.

The blood urges beat in Theuda's head, dragging tremors through him as he raised the crossed fingers at Corm. Immediately, the Tineman's men came striding in: so was the law followed without remorse and soon the tongue stood plumply out.

His corpse they put to the ravine that night and this was rightful.

Early the following day, under sombreness of drizzle, the Men of Scaur went to the forest in search of the true, intended Sorel. They found him, throat-slit and dead for no purpose; and he, a stranger, and Dillo of the Bank, they dressed in honour and together sent them forth in fire.

11

Grief stood in overrule within the Scaur and none more so than Theuda was kept in affliction of it. Nights went stared through to the blanching; and daylight, seeming at first relief, yet lay cumbersome about as the dark boding was sought to be passed by. Yet, over this, the month's sun bloomed and rose, drawing birdsong and early blossomburst with it, so reminding them that what had come had also gone. And it was this, the year enduring in its onward might, that soon had brought them from their desponding and out towards new honouring of the god by which they might seek to set matters aright.

As Tineman, Theuda went to this in added heights of fervour. Through the flat falls of morning light, he would lead out the parties to the hunt and daylong would strive, impatient of all ease and rest, anxious only for the intent of his aspiring. Nor could he find any sufficiency in this for then when the hunt was done, the ardency would have him rouse them yet further, to outbursts of praise – and later, with the drink and so far on into the night, to song and to a mirth all but maddened. From there, the dawn was close and waiting with its calls to new pursuit.

Kuno held himself like a hawk in the covert. Some were saying that the god had once more risen in strength into the Tineman; yet others murmured about the strange fury of his living and spoke with slow nods and worry pulling at their mouths. Kuno heard these things and, watching Theuda, hollow-hot of eye and caught up in his determination for joy, was fearful for him.

He also began to see how Acur too was now day after day in the forefront of the chase. There was skill in him and a certain headlong courage; but it was largely his zealousness and dogged energies that struck, such that it sometimes seemed as if he would rival Theuda himself.

Once when he had seen Acur in intense exchanges with Theuda, Kuno had words with him.

'The Tineman is much set about, Acur. He has no need of further invigoring.'

The man's look was beyond scrutiny, his voice sunk in its deepness.

'Set about?' he said. 'I should say rather that he is greatly impelled by the god's force at the moment. And that as such he has need of the support we can give him as companions. That is all I offer him. It seems better to me than the mere slighting of censure.'

Kuno hackled up but drew a hold on himself.

'There is no censure, Acur, as you well know. I only say that you have been urging him always further and that there is no wisdom in this. As his time grows nearer so do the burdens rest more heavily on him. As tanist, it is for me to warn you.'

Acur gave a smile and left. It was from this moment that he felt advised to go about his ways more secretly, taking care that Kuno should no longer see him with the Tineman. If Kuno now got to hear of Acur and his doings, it was mostly from Bobba who began to show himself stalwart and sharp-eyed in his concern.

'The Scaur and the Tineman's well-being above all, at whatever cost!' he would say to Kuno. And once, quietening his voice:

'Kuno, we should beware! Was there not some meaning in Corm's words of another being here for the women? And when one thinks of how much he and Acur were together – well, there could be danger there for Acur still keeps himself close to the Tineman.'

To this, Kuno could put no clear refuting. Yet both knew that, following the law of the Scaur, nothing could be brought against Acur without proof shown for it. However, agreement was made between them to watch him with utmost care. Later and privily, Kuno also brought Leudi and Ansi into this as well.

The hunting continued and so without relent. Far on into the month, the blood ran and worship bound them all; so that the women's denials passed but scarcely noticed. In all this, Theuda's leading was paramount and tireless. Only when he came back into the Scaur, torn about and messed with the excesses of death, did he seem freed from some of the testiness of his need. It was at one such moment of the day that Kuno chanced on him alone and made a broaching of his hidden fears.

'Rest?' replied Theuda. 'I need no rest. When the god's power comes among us, the Tineman must be there to guide.'

Kuno nodded and was grave in his pondering.

'Quite so,' he said. 'I had thoughts only for your health.'

Theuda looked sharply at him.

'I am well enough these days. I know what I can do.'

Kuno, thus thwarted, made a gesture of peace.

'I have spoken,' he said.

And so was seeming assurance given. Yet the very next day, as they made off for the hunt below an open sun, Kuno turned to greet Theuda, calling out; but the Tineman walked brushing past him, blind with his visions and unhearing.

For several days more, the sun kept clear. Out on the heights, brave winds blew and a brilliance lay settled over the forest. But then of a sudden all this fell away. The winds had passed and hazing and weight came into the sky so that suns went down in a dull reeking and, day and night, the air was thick and darkly still.

One morning early, Kuno stood waiting for Theuda at the falls. Gnat throngs hungered there upon the banks and he looked about with impatience for the Tineman's coming. The evening before, Theuda had not returned to the Scaur but had sent Eudo with the message for Kuno.

'I think perhaps he feels the need of time apart,' had added the older man. But then had stood there before Kuno as if with further words in him.

'What is it, Eudo?' asked Kuno.

'Nothing, it's nothing,' had answered Eudo and gone away quickly.

In those days of dour heat blocked in below the motionless, low-slung skies, it was as though a sickliness had come by stealth over the land. Everywhere among the dense pullulations of the spring forest, sound and movement had died away: it seemed that the very beasts themselves were laid low by some dread. And a sudden listlessness came into the men too so that they claimed a rest from the hunt and took to sitting about the Scaur, sweated and tense. It was during this stretch of torpor that Kuno heard mention of certain oddities and aberrant rantings that had been witnessed in Theuda in the past days. Nobody however could be got to speak much of these things – from loyalty and also from fear.

And so anxiety was part of the impatience in Kuno's waiting that morning at the falls.

But Theuda came. Purpose was in his striding and shows of perfection in his sureness of balance as he hastened down the steepness to the stream.

'Come!' he said but no smile was there.

And so he had turned and they were going. Far back across the forest they went before heading up towards a ridge; and Kuno could only marvel at Theuda's power of pace for the Tineman led by running, only slowing to climb the banks and rockways of the route. And he went as if to have gone by walking would have been burdensome, as if the speed were necessary to his body's ease.

They halted high, resting themselves haunched down upon the grass. Sky yellowed low and the stagnant air was packed damp about as they let their breathing settle. Far below, a long valley lay lifeless quiet.

The heat augmenting marked the growing day as Kuno blinked his heavy lids and watched the thoughts hardening in the Tineman's face. Theuda, working pebbles in his fist, was bent forward, grappled by effort.

Later, Theuda spoke up out of his silence.

'No,' he said. And then, to Kuno's dumbness: 'I am not coming back. I shall stay here.'

'Here?'

Theuda pointed towards a spiry stone set in the ground some way off.

'It was near the stone that Deor found me. It is there that I must now seek to regain myself.' And dismay made him roll his head. 'Kuno,' he said, 'again I feel the god's hold on me. By moments and days, it grows and fades; but always it strengthens. If I am to come as Tineman to the feast, I must find my way of standing clear of it.'

'You would fight the god? Here, alone?'

'Somehow, Kuno. The Scaur is all.'

It was in giving over the Scaur to Kuno's keeping that briefly Theuda's shoulders sank.

'Let them know,' he said, 'let them know that this is no breaking of trust. To have the assurance of their belief would stand me in good stead these coming days.'

And with that, the Tineman embraced his tanist and they went their separate ways.

As the month made on to its end, still rainless and with unbroken sulterings, despondency came increasingly to prevail within the Scaur. Among the men, the talk was much of the Tineman and his going from them: for now, after the fervour of those recent days, the lack of his leading in the hunt was felt most bitterly. And so it was that with this spirit of damaged hope, their talk often tended to other things.

One of them might say:

'Some bread would be good! Even an old crust.'

'Oh – and some cheese! With some fresh milk!'

Muttered groans came in answer; and so silence.

Then another, starting again:

'I could do with a woman, myself.'

'Ha! And in any case, you forget – in a few days' time the Hawthornmonth will be on us.'

And so silence once more.

And then later somebody might say:

'Well, I think the whole thing has gone on long enough. Surely Theuda would see it so if he were here.'

'And what would you suggest then?'

'We could come to an arrangement with them.'

'Or pretend to . . .'

'Huh! you young fellows are all the same! And where do you think that would get us? It would only end up as before.'

'Well, maybe – but at least there would be the chance of some different food and a good tup. All we do is just sit around here and talk about it.'

And so things would proceed till peevishly someone called an end to it. Yet for all this, the Scaur's resolve remained held; for in truth, beyond their spleenful words, the trusting of belief lay ever strong.

Kuno took roasted flesh to Theuda and spoke with him. There were few words in the Tineman and a farness had grown into his eyes; but he urged Kuno, telling him to keep up strength – for the coming of the Hawthornmonth was bound to bring new hope.

'You will see,' he said. 'They will take heart; for the season of preparation will put them in mind of the feast. And then I shall be back amongst you all and made whole once more.'

It was with the new month opening that Kuno next came to the ridge. Up on top, he palmed the slime of closeness from his forehead and looked about into the glare. Later, still alone, he began calling too – but only his voice was there in the massive quiet; and beside him, the great stone rising thick and sure.

Noon was well past when, down on a plot of barrenness beyond the ridge where scrub and occasional, stubborn trees sprang parched and thin, he at last found the Tineman. Hunched and head down he sat, there below a flowering gean, with arms pulled tight about his knees. Kuno, touching him, gave a gasp at the chillness of his flesh; and only then did the Tineman's head come slowly up.

'You – you were sleeping . . .' said Kuno in a voice quavered by alarm.

Chafings were roughened dark on Theuda's cheeks and a wealed gash ran messily into his hair. Though the look of stunning was upon him, a violent brightness pricked in his eye. He swallowed painfully and was struggling. Then he spoke with measure:

Far and each moment
Yet further!
By day and night,
Wings of force
Have descent
On me:
There is no space
Beyond the strength.

Kuno sat down.

'Theuda, let me send someone – Leudi or Ansi perhaps. They could be of help to you.'

Understanding of this seemed to have escaped Theuda. He stayed toiled in silence, his fixed eyes showing nothing but the buried fire. But then suddenly, bursting kecked through clamped teeth, words came again:

Rend, rend
And make!
Alone
I wage myself
On utterness
And dismay.
No man
Shall stand for
Another's fight.

All afternoon, they sat beneath the whitening of the gean and Theuda spoke, locked in his words. Growled and gagged up they came; but then, gradually unbound, they grew to run as an eagre from him, always gathering, till Kuno no longer had sense or cognizance of their coming. He sought to bring some calm on Theuda; but, unawares, Theuda spoke over him and made always on. And in his speaking, it began to appear that, among the turmoiled vehemence, there was rising and again a repeated thing, a thing of urgency that Kuno was to know: namely, that somehow and as yet but poorly formed, there was opening for Theuda a new understanding of the

Scaur, a clarity that would show all of strength and failure and so was to give them the way of entrance to a security of greatness beyond.

Kuno heard it all. Then, giving pledges of the Men of Scaur's continuing belief, he went from Theuda and took himself back along the ridge. Past and beyond the stone he went and so down into the heat-laden forest again. There, out of sight of beast and sky, he turned his face against a rock and wept for his friend's crazing. For a while, misery and horror shuddered from him; but when it had passed, he ran on and, reaching the crossing by the falls, he stripped himself and plunged head-long into the yeasted and cleansing waters of the hills.

Suns fell and always into thickness; and the moon, coming risen to full, rode out rufous and bodeful.

It was by dawn after this that she came again, the girl child, her voice floating bell-bright up from the forest below. They went down to her and she stood there before them, shyly, and said:

'Who is the tanist among you? I am to speak with him.'

When Kuno came forward, she beckoned him apart. Then she reached up and he felt her warm breath blowing on his ear.

'The Tineman is finished,' she whispered. 'Be done with him and hold the Scaur yourself. It is the only way now.'

Kuno sprang up. And with that, harelike, the girl ran off.

'Come back!' he shouted. But her laughter, ringing high with the fun of it, was already fading among the trees.

Immediately, the men pressed round. But Kuno was short with them and took himself off alone.

Some way into the forest quiet, he had halted, smacking at a tree in the annoyance of his puzzlement, when he heard foot-steps softly behind him. He turned scowl-faced in his thoughts.

'What is it, Bobba? Can it wait?'

The fat man leaned forward and his lips were rounded with secrecy.

'Kuno!' he said in an urgent undertone. 'Somebody is pass-ing words to the women!'

Kuno came up close to him.

'So it would seem,' he said and paused. 'But how could you know of this?'

Advantage smiled harshly in Bobba's face.

'I also know who and how,' he said somewhat coyly. Then touched Kuno on the arm. 'Let you and I go to the hunt late this afternoon,' he said. 'Then you will see.'

After the mystification of the child's visit, there were some glances in the Scaur that day and a certain edge in manner. But then further consternation was brought upon them; for later, as they all chanced to be gathered together again, Bobba suddenly spoke up loudly to Kuno:

'It is tonight then that you will tell us?' he said. 'About what you have decided.'

To which Kuno, without comprehension yet quickly alert, broke swiftly free of his pause and answered:

'Why, yes! I see no gain in waiting longer.'

As they left the Scaur in the slow decline of day, Kuno upbraided Bobba for this.

'Why did you have to speak up so? It is not right that the tanist should seem to play games with the Scaur.'

'There was no other way,' answered Bobba lightly. 'We needed it – to draw him out. You will see.'

Out in the forest, Bobba urged care and quiet and then led them back till they stood by the upsheering of rock below the Scaur. Here they withdrew into a dark thicket and lodged themselves.

'And now we wait!' breathed Bobba with his secret, knowing smile.

About them, the day flagged and fell away, giving over into a humid afterlight where only the call of birds lay on the air. It was then that Bobba signed towards the cliff rim of the Scaur; and Theuda, craning up, saw a shadowed figure come out on to the edge. A moment later, the missel song came fluting down, long and in its turn, sinuously smooth. When it paused, there rose from the medley bird noises of the bush an answering thrush, singing clear up over all the evening's still.

144

For a while, they crouched and gave ear to this hidden interchange and Bobba's head was cocked and questioning as he watched Kuno. But finally Kuno leaned forward.

'We'll take the lower bird!' he breathed.

They crept, easing always towards the song sound. Near to it, Bobba went wide, encircling. Soon Kuno could make out the warbling shape but as he poised himself to leap, a noise elsewhere preceded him. At this, the shape swung round, eye-white in alarm, and burst across his lunge to flee. In pursuit, Kuno was fast and closing when suddenly he went, his foot snagged away and himself diving to be jounced against a tree.

Bobba sped past but soon came trotting back.

'I lost her,' he said. 'She was too quick for me.'

In the Scaur, the pitch flares were alight and everyone up in spirit.

'Hey, Kuno! Do you feel it?' called Brun, gesturing to the soft plucks of a wind that was rising from the south.

'Perhaps we will get some rain now,' said Uhtred, kicking at the dust. 'Just look at those cracks!'

'No rain on that wind,' said Beohrt glumly.

'How do you always manage to see things on the bright side?' said Fer from beyond him.

Everyone laughed.

'Well, you can smell it,' retorted Beohrt, ignoring the laughter. 'Damp all right – but there's no rain there.'

Kuno came up and broke into this.

'Men of Scaur!' he said loudly and the lightness was cut from them by the intent of his voice. 'I call a meeting! There are things to be said.'

Knocking of wind in the flares threw uncertainty over the men as they stood about Kuno. When he spoke, he had all the bite of scorn and disgust in his words.

'Yet again,' he began, 'yet again has some vileness been found amongst us!' Feet and voices stirred. 'For a year now, each happening of moment in the Scaur has been sent in report to the women of the holm. Theuda himself had some sense of this yet could find nothing sure. Only today has it come clear. Now, as tanist, I bring the accusation before you . . . You may stay, Acur!' he called out as the figure shifted in search of shadow.

The man stood turned on the boundary of light, affecting surprise.

'Yes, Acur! You, the singer of songs, warblewhistler, birdmaster! All that fine piping! I accuse you – of words passed covertly and from our very midst, words that have put the secrecy of the Scaur at risk and have given strength over to the women when we stand at loggerheads with them.'

To this, Acur turned full-square and spoke pityingly from his height.

'Do not do this to yourself, Kuno! You, the tanist who must soon come in as Tineman and ruling friend to all – do not bring ruin upon yourself by such madness. Long has the Scaur been luckless and lost. We all know this . . .' Here angered calls broke out all around and swept the speech away from him. 'But,' he went on, raising his words, 'do not think, because of this, to make of me the victim of your fears. Look rather to the weak and fanciful behaviour of him who should have led us clear.' And ending sharp and loud above the swell of talk, he cried: 'Listen to me, Men of Scaur! The Tineman is finished! His mind has broken loose!'

Semblances of restraint fell apart. Clamoured curse and questioning broke out in assault on Acur; but he stood firm and gave back strong assertions of his words. Wind gusting and running among the flares could but spread confusion further.

Kuno leaped forward as if touched by a cautery.

'Guile!' he shouted as he came to Acur; and, with this, the hackled crowding of noise began to abate. 'Sheer guile! See how quickly you speak of other things so as to try and turn the charge. But I have accused and you shall give me answer by the law. Again I put it to you – have you not been the one passing word to the women all these months? And was the song of birds not the means of this betrayal?'

146

Acur looked at him and shook his head as if disbelieving.

'To speak by bird cry? Why, that indeed would be ingenious! But even if this were possible, to whom should a man address himself in such a strange and wonderful tongue?'

'Acur, your dissembling is of no gain to you. You know well – the language would only be spoken to another so skilled. A woman of the holm perhaps.'

'Your words have as much worth as a dog's dreaming,' answered Acur with bitterness. 'The Men of Scaur will want proof, Kuno. I warned you – you shall suffer for this.'

'Not so,' retorted Kuno. 'They shall have their proof. Bobba here stands witness for me. He it was who was with me this evening when we all but caught the other bird.'

Light and unresting shadow moved on Bobba's face.

'It was so,' he said without feeling. 'It was just as Kuno says.'

Acur looked long at Bobba.

'May the god himself forgive you, Bobba!' he said at length.

Now suddenly the Men of Scaur would have no more of this. Eudo it was who called out dark and rough in voice:

'You admit it then?'

'If you will . . .' said Acur easily.

And so they rose as one against him in his shamelessness, shouting abuse and scorn, and would willingly have taken vengeance without more ado. Yet Acur heard them unperturbed and spoke back sure and smirkingly:

'I demand to have the Tineman's word on this. It is my right. Without his consent, you can do nothing to me.'

And, in truth, his claim for this was by entitlement of law. Accordingly, Kuno gave orders that he was to be taken and set apart in the great hut.

'And make him fast!' he said. 'We want no further trouble from him.'

So they bound his hands and, putting a halter about his neck, ran the rope over the stout ridge-tree of the roof, fastening it to his ankles so that a pace either way would put a throttle on him. Then, closing the door, they left him to the darkness.

All evening, protractions of their dismay and pain held the Men of Scaur in debate. Even when the violence and shame had been put aside, a greater dread came upon them.

'What if he is right?' said Brun. 'What if the Tineman really is crazed?'

'And if he is not strong enough to lead us at the feast,' added Gort, 'what then?'

Kuno strove to calm them.

'It is a fool who trusts in Acur's word,' he countered. 'He would say anything if it was to his need.'

'Then why did he grin in such sureness?' came back Brun. 'Tell me that! Was it not because he knew himself safe? Because he knew the Tineman to be beyond the giving of the law?'

Scuffles of argument broke out. Then Uhtred spoke.

'Kuno, we need to know for sure how the Tineman stands. The uncertainty of this is a shackle on everything we do.'

Kuno nodded.

'Theuda lives close to the god these days,' he replied carefully, 'and this is hard for us to follow. But if we cannot stand by him in this with trust, how should we expect him to come through it so as to lead us at the feast?'

Quiet acceptance of this was given by all.

'We shall still need a judgement on Acur,' reminded Fer.

'And then what about our numbers?' said Beohrt, coming forward. 'Have you forgotten that? Soon we shall be short by two.'

Much discussion followed, some saying that the numbers must be made up at all costs while others voiced fears that any new men might well have been prepared by the women to give trouble.

At this, Bobba put forward his view.

'Now that the last weakness has been uprooted,' he said, 'surely it would be better for all in this time of stress that we remain strong and few – rather that than risk more trouble. After all,' he added, 'when the feast is past, things may well be different.'

By the count of hands, they quickly came to agreement with him on this.

'But the women?' called out Witu then. 'Do we any longer know what they have in mind? Are we even sure that they will come to the mountain at Ura?'

Once again, orderless shouts and clashing started up; for the doubt over this was unthinkable.

'He could tell us!' cried Brun, thumbing towards the hut. 'I'd vouch that he knows exactly what they are up to!'

'You would hardly get much out of him,' put in Bobba.

'Oh, he would talk all right – if we bent him a bit.'

New ferment of vengefulness began to heat up among the men. But Kuno called a close on this, saying that there would indeed be a time for such things – but not before judgement was given.

It was later, as they went off to the huts, that Uhtred faced Kuno.

'You did not answer my question earlier,' he said. 'About Theuda.'

'And what would you have had me say then?' responded Kuno with all the bite of desperation. 'Should I have told the men the truth – that they are to live these coming days by hope alone, that in truth I have no inkling of how the Tineman really stands?'

All night long, the wind blew warm and loud about the Scaur. No rain fell with it but when, by early light, it veered and settled north of west, it brought clearing skies and a new dryness in the air. Day broke with fierce brilliance.

Gort, going to the hut with provisions for Acur, shouted to the others to come. And they, as they ran in jostling through the door, were halted dumb. For there, with his belly scraping low upon the floor, hung Acur, bowed arching head and heel up on the rope of his tethering.

Theuda was slow and his arms limp beneath the startling beat of the sun. He made shuffles in the dust and ringed about on tracks worn among the tussocks. Now and then he shook his head and turned off to wade among the bushes where prickly sprigs tore idly at him. Nick and slash, some caked over, netted his legs. His clothes lay somewhere else.

Words of his thoughts were working as goads on him. The patterns of the sounds kept shaping up, this way and that. Dogging at them, he made trial of each for it to fit: took here and then from there and put that aside for another or perhaps yet another for its sudden seeming rightness. Yet by the by, he sloughed them all. And then the very vapour of his thinking was forming anew.

He had to find his saying of it – that he knew.

Darkness and light passing had happened. And then, once, he was walking and somehow it was with him, almost as if from before. And to speak it out clear, to make structures of it, to try and show up its intent – that too was of his need. Before, words had just been. Now, for this, it was not so and they were there only if trapped or quarried or dreamed for his purpose. And he strove: always, always growth and a promise of breaking forth seemed just at hand. Yet there was no time: he lived in a terror of sleep.

When he walked, frails of food were often at his feet. He stepped round them mostly but sometimes he crouched down and played with the flies and white hives for a while and it seemed to give some order and ease to the struggle of his words. One day even, a fresh bowl was pressed under his chin and a loud voice came out of it; but it was nothing, it had no purpose for him whatsoever.

By night, it grew greater. To begin with, he would sit staggered down somewhere or stand clutching at a tree. Then he tried to walk with the words and the night would sprawl him into thickets and make to split his head on the rock. At this, he would just lie there, sometimes clean through to the first gleaming, face down, with the tangle and earth held for surety while the enormousness worked on in him.

Theuda stood in the bushes and mouthed dead sounds. The grasp of it all was so close yet was nowhere sure or fixed; so he made more words of what it might be, hoping to force it into a truth. He snatched hold of the leafage and strained on it and all the while his feet padded about.

Then there was a man in front of him. He tugged further at the bush and went on with his words but strangely the man was still there. In fact, he was much closer and speaking a question time and again:

'What is it? What is happening?'

And with that, of a sudden, the words of the days came out into the light and streamed into the first speaking of his truth:

kraw   kraw

tseetsee

     prheeh

  pee-ach tootoo

     toopiuww

cier!

   cier!

        gyeeh

tsilidiudiu

    tink   tink

      pruir!

pruir!

   pruir! tsili kra

kra

juep peu juep

tpik

    kra   fuuet

kraw

When the man shook his head, Theuda said the words again. And then once more, with carefully measured beat for the man's patent dullness. But the man went away.

Theuda stood there picking thoughtfully at the crop of thorns in his hand. The man was quite gone from his mind.

After a while, he snuffled the slime from his nose and went off slowly to the tussocks with his words.

Day after day, the skies kept domed out, merely rimmed with the smoke of heat, as the sun tracked dazzlingly over. Barebellies were again suddenly about and wherever the men might go, it was as if they could not escape the spirit power of them.

'But why should we feel menaced by them?' said Beohrt. 'They do nothing.'

Yet it was so: it was as if the very power of fruitfulness were being drawn up both as a reminder and a threat to them all. And the unease of this made the men now consider it ill to meet with a barebelly – so that many a mishap or strange turn of fortune came to be ascribed to such an encounter.

All the while, Kuno deepened steadily in his lying. He found ways of concealment and contrived words to bring renewed hope to the Men of Scaur. Even to Uhtred he managed the shape of a smile.

'I was wrong in my uncertainty,' he said. 'Now each day the Tineman finds further power. All will soon be well.'

But the pain of this, of what was to be held secret bore hard on him. Yet he could see no other way.

It was in the last part of the month, but twenty days from the feast itself, that Kuno went out from the Scaur yet again. Weighed under by his thoughts, he made on through the long forest ways and began his climb.

High up, where the trees thinned out to the bareness of the ridge, he felt the sun sear smack at his shoulders. And now he began to tread more slowly, with a waning resolve, for his meetings with the Tineman had come to be things of horror and loathing to him.

He walked in a stealth of listening. Overhead, raven and falcon were at spar; back beyond, whistles and the zee-zee of smaller birds rose from the forest edge. On the ridge rising before him, heat held firm and still among the manged growth of the brush.

And now as he went, a dark shadowing of expectancy was

with him, an apprehension that put the prickle of chill over his skin and caused his going to be checked by hesitance and much sensing about. When he entered the brush, he quickly took to moving with careful changes of pace and line, fast and turning and doubling and then halting even in his stride. For now he was sure of it – another was there, close and without either lenience or fellow-feeling for him.

He heard it too late, the pad-pad-pad of gathering speed in the dust behind him. His half-turn saw but the teeth and the bursting-tight eyes among overcrusts of dirt and blood before the blow came. But sheer grace of body brought his arm up to take it and faster yet he threw across a twofold swing of fist and elbow that spun the other's force on from him.

But he knew: Kuno knew and was gone. Fleetness took him by bounds away and, clearing the scrub mass, he sped on down the length of ridge to the forest cover.

Throughout the afternoon, the blast of heat stoked hard upon the heights. It was well on, with the sun dropped low and a steady softening now settled in, that Kuno came edging up once again. Skirting the bushes of the top, he stole a way across the flank of hill towards where the stone stood spearing black into the sky.

Noises were there. Quickly he stepped in among the rocks and slunk catwise on to come peering through a crack of boulder block.

By the stone, the dust of the earth was scored by a host of circling shapes. Ring abutted on ring, was interlocked and lined out across the ground singly and by the tens and hundreds. Among them, stamping start-naked and yard-stiffened, messed over and sinewed taut in his frenzy, troated the Tineman.

12

And now with the days almost lengthened out to full, the shortfall of rain and the towering heat had begun to put their mark on the forest. Shallow of root or just starved out on steep slopes, weak growth everywhere showed clear, with leaves crimped sapless and rustling to the touch. In any stretch of open, beyond the trees, the grass lay scorch-stunted and widely undercut by meshworks of cleft and fracture. And over all rose screens of dazing air thrown up by rock plate and packed earth alike, kiln-hot under the steady height of the sun. Streams wormed hollow, dust scuffed up and choked, a taint of rot hung lightly about. It was thus that the Oakmonth came in, heavy and hard to bear.

It was under the force of this that the Men of Scaur finally broke from Kuno's holding of them.

'No!' they shouted. 'No more! These are words, just words!'

'Forty days he has been from us, Kuno. No one can say we have not shown trust.'

'But now we need him. The feast is close.'

And when, yet again, Kuno sought to turn them with the comfort of assurances, they cried out over his speech with violent scoutings.

'Bring him back!' they called and refused to hear him further.

It was leadened with misgiving that Kuno set out the following morning. He had bidden Leudi and Ansi go with him, saying that they would leave early before the others were about. As they made ready in the cool light, Kuno said to them:

'You had best bring ropes.' And when they looked at him, he added: 'One never knows.'

They travelled fast for now Kuno had a mind to see the matter through with the Men of Scaur. The sun came up clear and had soon taken away the last flinders of night cloud; and by the time they reached the foot of the ridge, the full fire of day was in the sky.

'Wait for me here,' said the tanist. 'If I have need of you, you will hear my call.'

All was quiet. At the stone, the circles lay teeming still; and just beyond, Kuno came to a dip where the grass was torn about and scabs of sun-baked vileness dotted the ground. But of Theuda, he saw nothing.

When he found him, it was quite to his amazement. In a thicket bed he lay, among bine and leaf and the mottles of light, and his breathing was deep in a trough of sleep. Bone showed sharp on him and he was torn and wallowed all over – but a purity of ease shone in his face such that Kuno could only sit and marvel.

The sun arched out and rose and at last Kuno touched the Tineman on the shoulder.

'Kuno!' Theuda sat up slowly; then saw himself. 'I . . .'

Kuno smiled.

'We shall go down to the falls,' he said. 'There is still good water there. Here now, give me your hand.'

Theuda's body was spent. But Leudi and Ansi came up and together they brought him down off the ridge and so by stages the group made its way back across the forest. In the stillness of noon, with the falls sluicing through bright air into shade below, Theuda cleansed himself of the days of his struggle and then turned for the Scaur in the fulfilment of his dream.

Inquiry and triumphs of relief were about and there above him with birds in the sunlight. He heard fellowship everywhere and reached out towards it for he was still largely beyond speaking. Later, they took him to a hut on the edge of the Scaur that he might be alone with his thoughts in his resting; and there, when he had eaten, he closed his eyes and so too did the darkness collapse opening beneath him.

He woke briefly in the owl-light and lay staring at the shape of memory. Elsewhere in the Scaur, there were sounds but his closer awareness was so vast that they were not part of him. And then suddenly, in a snap, he was asleep again and the awareness had shifted but slightly and as it grew, he was drifting ever nearer to what was at its heart. When next he awoke, Kuno was standing in the doorway and the sun was shining out of his head.

Rest and food soon brought Theuda up to steadying once more though the printmark of rib and bone was still strong on his meagred body. The Men of Scaur were much about him and with solicitude; yet for all this there was a certain hanging back and when they spoke it was with a quietness of care.

'They say it is something in your look,' said Kuno. 'I think it unnerves them.'

And indeed as he slipped his enfeeblement, Theuda had now come to live in the light of a power that was of calm and sureness and joy. No longer was he bent by the making of words: it was as if he had passed on beyond, as if the delivering of what was his truth had come through resplendent to the very surface of his being. He shone, they said, and it was of this that they went in awe, speaking of it as the mark of the god himself.

And such was it, so bright and unfaltering, that sleep and rest seemed quite gone from him: by night now, he sat alone and always it was there with him. And so too was the clarity that had brought him to see his way forward to the feast – a thing of wonder and utterness for himself and of glory proper to a Tineman of the Scaur.

Far on one night, under star glint and still warmth, Theuda came to his tanist and called him from his sleep.

'Come!' he said urgently. And as they went apart from the huts: 'There are things that you must know.'

It was then, in the pit of darkness lying before dawn, that Theuda spoke to Kuno of the feast and of what was to come to be for the Scaur when he was gone.

'Kuno,' he began, 'as friend and tanist, hear me now! The days run on and still the Scaur stands unsure.'

'We grow stronger though,' asserted Kuno, speaking with words gruff from sleep. 'Since Acur chose to put an end to himself, we have at last come clear of all such treachery. Soon we shall be returned to strength in full.'

For a moment, there was only the greatness of dark about. Then:

'It was not as you think,' said Theuda. 'Quite otherwise, in fact. Acur was killed.'

Roiled up in anger of dismay and disbelief, Kuno came back at this with many questions and objecting doubt. But Theuda shook his head and could give him neither his manner nor means of knowing it; nor moreover even who had done the deed.

'There was a day when suddenly the knowledge was part of me,' was all that he could say. 'It was up there by the stone.' But then, returning to his purpose, he went on: 'I tell you, Kuno, just as these flaws of dissent and deceit are with us now so will they remain till the Scaur has found new ways. As Tineman, it will be for you to bring these in.'

'What new ways?'

'Listen to me,' said Theuda with sudden fervour. 'Is it not so that both our failing within and our struggle to keep peace outside the Scaur have to do with the women of the holm?'

Kuno gave his grunt of assent.

'Then perhaps it is with them that we should look for change. Perhaps the way we are just here to honour the god is not enough . . .'

'That is an ugly thing to say!' broke in Kuno.

Theuda laughed: his sureness was strong.

'I mean only that all of us here, enclosed in the Scaur and given over solely to the god, that this has no making of strength in it. We live without balance as it were – and in a vanity of content.'

'What else would you have but the god and us? Truly,

157

Theuda, for a Tineman you have an unhappy way of speaking!'

Theuda let the night come calm over them before he spoke again.

'Remember,' he said, 'I too chose the Scaur. Here I have found the god and all the joy of comradeship. I have no cause to speak against it. I have only its well-being in mind.'

'Then leave it be!' replied Kuno curtly. 'Its fortunes will mend soon enough.'

'You believe that? Even as we are now? With yet another among us a felon, unknown? With us staying short in number rather than risk new men? I tell you, Kuno, something is lacking! A change must be made!'

'The women?' said Kuno, flaring in amazement. 'You mean, after all this, you would have them here?'

'No,' said Theuda, 'not necessarily that. But some sharing of sorts, yes – and a proper understanding, a working together. We cannot just scorn them – they are part of us. Your own mothers are among them!'

'But they are different, the women!'

'Maybe. Yet still we need them.' He paused. 'And anyway, to set together things equal in difference, is this not to make something of strength?'

But Kuno answered this in a voice from far off.

'What are you talking about? These are words that have no meaning for me.'

The weighted enormity of night had already softened to tingeing when the two men parted. With all the contrivances of mockery and persuading speech, Kuno had gone to his utmost in striving against the aberrancies of Theuda's belief. He spoke to him of the very principles of the Scaur and its ways; he gave citings of guidance in the words of Deor and of Saer before him; he made mention of the Tineman's story, with its warning about the people overruled by women long ago.

'Warning?' Theuda had replied. 'But warnings are of danger; and danger speaks of fear and unease. If we of the Scaur regard the women with such scorn then perhaps it is a fear of them that lies concealed in our hearts.'

Kuno could only laugh. But Theuda went on and now with all the vigour of his truth in him:

'We should not forget, Kuno, that god or no god, in the end there is no Scaur without the women. The power of life is all.'

Kuno had fallen silent. And now Theuda was murmuring to himself.

'Strength is Beauty! Seed is Hope!'

As the night passed to its close, Kuno knew that his words had gone without avail. There was such poised might of belief in Theuda, such a blind urgency of need to give over to the Scaur what had come to him that at last, as if relenting, Kuno feigned assent and went from him.

It had been Theuda's way to tell his tanist of these things first; but now he was to speak of them to the Men of Scaur as a whole. Even as day broke, Kuno went secretly to each of them.

'His time alone has turned his head somewhat,' he said. 'Have no fear though – he is fit and well. But humour him for the feast is close.'

All that day, under the huge heat, Theuda sat among his friends and spoke of the discovery of his truth, telling them how it might be of counsel to the Scaur. Stippled with sweat and his eyes widened in belief, the words of his happiness came forth from him and the men smiled and nodded their heads in seeming wonder and agreement.

It was early in the evening that Kuno, walking alone in the forest, met with a group of barebellies bearing bread and milk and meal. Greeting him, they said that a truce was to be held for the season of the feast; for this was only rightful. Kuno thanked them warmly and sent words of friendship to Ead and all the women of the holm. Then, hurrying back lightfooted with all the relief of hope, he went to Theuda with the news.

In the hut, he found the Tineman crouched down in the shadows with his arms drawn tight about his head in pain.

The fleaming in his head and the stunned reeling had stricken him before. Up by the stone.

He said this but immediately was gone again, back into the

silence of clenching where there was but nothing else.

Later, Kuno came with sops of bread and fresh milk and Theuda ate, hunkered low and puckered about the face. But not long after, in the thickest of last light, he staggered up at the foul rising in him and held on to the doorpost as it came, fountaining out into the dark.

The days followed on with the forest still and full of the hauntings of cuckoo call. Up high, there was always blue and blindburst but otherwise chalky hazes muffled all. In this time the Men of Scaur lived quiet and alone: the hunt was closed and they were much in preparation for what was to come.

For Kuno, the women's easing of manner had brought new assurance.

'You see,' he said to Theuda, 'it will all come right. We have only to stand by our belief. In the end, they will see the sense of it.'

'It means nothing,' muttered Theuda, his words pushed past clamped teeth. 'It is merely to lull you so that you see strength where there is none.' And later, repeatedly: 'Ead. I must see Ead. Get me Ead.'

At which Kuno would calm him and make as if messages had already been sent.

But the worsening grew over Theuda. Now he would have nothing of the light and kept himself in the stifle of darkness, crouched down with his head pushing back and back against the stiffening of his neck. There was an oddness in him too that made for testy outbursts and a rage when he was thwarted.

'Where is she?' he would shout. 'How many more times do I have to ask?'

'We are still waiting for her,' Kuno would answer. And then later when he could no longer say this with conviction: 'She has refused, Theuda. She will not come.'

'No! Tell her that we will talk, that she was right! Tell her to come! She must!'

And once again Kuno would make a promise of his lie and

feel the loathing of this deception: yet he knew that the Scaur was to be held before all.

Sometimes, between the ringings of pain, Theuda would talk lengthily, speaking of this and that from among memory and hope. It was mostly to the darkness, though he spoke too when Kuno was there but often this was quite without any acknowledgement of him. And then suddenly he would break off and fall back to the grinding of his jaw, his hands clasped about his head, with all the rocking to ease his neck. Food was still beyond his holding, force spouting of vomit seizing him each time; and his breech and legs were messed, with sourness and black trails. Kuno had seen too that the eyes had gone cast and the mouth drawn up twisted to one side.

The men were kept from all this. They heard only that the Tineman now lay in the extremes of closeness with the god and knew that this was to be of their rejoicing. In order that he should have strength to lead them at the feast, he was to remain apart and Kuno was to take on the holding of the Scaur once more.

It was as the sun went out of the sky on the eve of Ura that Gort came in from the forest. Matters of some moment seemed to hasten him in his going; yet he passed quietly by the gathering of men and on into the early shadows of the edge.

'Theuda!' he whispered as he slipped into the dark of the Tineman's hut. 'Theuda, their man – it is Bobba!'

The dream had passed into the quiet and he was still standing. He felt the fire all over him, lily-light and unquenchable; and above, a chasm opening into vast ways. He moved a bit and the fire rippled on him; and breathed deeply so that his chest seemed to throw out licks of its flaming. And when he made silent words, it was as if a stream of power poured from his mouth. And then he knew, that of course it had always been and that hitherto only uncertainty had kept him from it.

He put in small pacings along the wall. Now and then, he

would stop and say her name in a mouthful of flames. And so he would go on, marking the paces and only staggering slightly when the darkness was suddenly blasted by the rush of light. Then he would stay down, hunched against the wall, letting its echoes sound through and through him: for it was the power and soon he was to bear the honouring himself.

The pains had quietened in his head. The previous day had been busy with them, the call of the horn at the mark of dawn finding him writhed and choking on groans. Among this, he had struggled with thoughts of the men and their hope; and later, when he heard the cries of laughter and the fire crackle, he had been drawn to being with them and the feast. So that when Kuno had come, he had stepped forward with a determination to eagerness; but at that, a force had locked on him such that he fell sacklike and lay briefly without abilities in either limb or tongue. After this, the day passed long with its rigours. Between the bouts, he could only hold himself weakened out of mind and dulled to the revelling close by.

The brilliance darkened away into night. For an instant, he was left leaning over voids of dismay. But as trust caught him up again, he was pacing on, straining against the slowness of the night and all that still lay imponderable before him. At times, randomness of memory flitted troubling out on his edges. Faces came and suddenly presentiments of some horror; but none of it fell into shape or sense and soon it too had gone, fading on the drift of thought. But for all this, her name was never far from him.

Later, he made another step and the day had begun. The fire on him had steadied and he saw now how a mere drawing up of muscle would set motions in it; so much so that when at last they came, he called out to them in warning. But though the cry itself billowed in flurrying flame, the two tall ones calmly took hold of him.

He was carried out and so on down under the plains of dawn and into shadowed places where he could see trunks rising up to nothing among hanging leaf and the flakes of sky. And then they too were there above him with faces bent over, the two and the other one, and he was sinking away from them with coolness reaching up to take weight from his body. And suddenly they were no more and he was apart and buried in the drumming with swarms of bubbles tickling across his face.

He opened his mouth and drank swiftly. But it tasted heavy and rich and the bubbles and the water sound had quite gone. Now there was only heat and the closed-off dark among stillness; and when he turned, a tree that struck him.

Somewhere a voice said:

'Let him rest. There's time yet.'

He turned quickly, intending to surprise the voice. But the encumbrance of his head dragged at him and he lurched. And when he peered about from out of the dark, he saw only stretches of scorched grass and the ring of stones.

He ambled off and was alone somewhere among the packing of branches. The fire was flaring strongly again and, in a sudden fret at holding it, he reared up and trod on the air with the hoofs of his hands. Afterwards, when it had settled, he just stood there, idly rubbing against a bough with the beam of his hornwork: for now his greatness lay on him with all the weight of a massive peace.

When the tall ones touched him, he went, seeping fire, and put himself close to the great stone. There were others about but the greetings they called to him and the chanting they later set up seemed as neither here nor there: for already he was alone and going forth along ways of gladness and greater darkening.

A hand came with things to chew. And when he was back in the place with the branches, they brought him a bowl and with it a hare. But he was resolute and refused to do it, using stealth instead to let it go. At this, they grew angry but he turned from them and was already busy elsewhere.

Of a sudden, the pains were in his head again. He grunted and clawed at them and started bringing up slime and looseness from his belly. Bird cry nearby pierced him and became howl sounds that were so beyond his bearing that he could only beat the earth and bite at scattered cones. But when at last it had passed away again, such a clearness came into him that his purpose then seemed almost to hand. He hoofed the dust and sidled a bit; and as the sense of his greatness grew overmastering, the ring of stones surrounded him and he was ramping up in his magnificence over those who were there.

He alone was the god! He alone!

Now the stones had quite gone. Trees came and fell behind and he was going up clear of them, climbing on slopes that would take him to the way in from the heights. Heat pressed down, hags and tumblestones were underfoot; only the shadow of the other paced beside. Here he might pause or fall but there was to be no hindering and snarls of his intent rang in his throat.

Sun hanging high by noon was shining among breezes on the peak. He gasped and was wolfing them and arching back against his neck. But suddenly he was going into totters: for the forest, distantly below, was on the tilt and moving off. Words were beside him and he clutched at them for support. But when the forest movements ceased, they were still there and would not stop. So he made to force them away. But they became shouts and something slipping under his snout pressed a clot of wetness into his mouth. He snorted and hawked against it but already it had burst in his gullet and gone.

Later, there was only silence and the stepway falling in wavers below him. Down out of day he came edging. Cold air played strangely from the slit in the rock and he drew breath in deep to feel the fire expanding. Once more, swaying, he knew her name:

'Alphito!'

And with that, he and the darkness became one.

He snuffled at the smell and the lust came troating out of him. The sound separated itself and moved off among cavities of grey and black light. Wall blocks and the trap of funnel forms boomed it back and then it was larger and about

164

in great numbers. Everywhere, even from far above in the upper chambers, the herds gave answer.

The path turned steeper. It slid about and tried to escape him but he trod on it firmly and followed down, his breath now slowing, now coming to pace again. Peering out, he saw the darkness blackening away over a ladderlike fall in the rock with water gushes and great spaces of void hidden below. He chewed on his mouthful of noises and then slowly began to lower himself down. But his hoofs could get no holding and he swung his head from the sudden buzz of rage at this, rattling the rock with his antlers. He tried other ways but always the slithering was there under him. Groans began to wedge in his throat and he disgorged them raucously so that everything thickened with the mobbing of them. And then when the smell came to him again and hunger joined in with the raging, he shuffled round and stepped clear out into the dark.

Freedom was suddenly everywhere. He walked and struggled with it but the kicks and spinning flails he made were of little use and only skidded about on the rush of air. Yet a grin bared his teeth as he went. And even when the shingle bed came up and clubbed him across the hind-quarters, he only grunted at the blow. He eased himself up off his haunches and, splashing through the water, headed towards where some lesser darkness showed.

Once, clattering in halls without edges, he was rolled over and lay trying to tear the sharpnesses out of his head. For a while, he barked with it and the sound became enormous and fearsome. Later, he was still there and now in the quiet, seeking about to find the up and the down of things.

Darkness was massive before him yet somewhere in it there was a perfect roundness, brimful of light. He went towards it but it was already moving from him; and then when he craftily turned with it, it was coming back and suddenly rushing at him. A hoof caught and as the round-ness reached him, he tripped and went headlong into it.

The roundness was long as well and fell away under his

steps. There was a troating in it too that kept bounding on down ahead so that he went maddened and staggering with his speed to catch it. As soon as he stopped though, it went; and he would creep a little, making up on it. But the moment he put out challenges, it was there again.

Colour was changing among this and the roundness spun so that he was pacing sometimes on his head, sometimes on the flat of his belly. And often when he made to tread forward, the roundness under him was not at all where he thought it to be so that his hoof went clean past it; and then he would stay lurched at rest, tapping his forehead to knock away the idling of the pain. And all the time, the great length of the roundness was piling up on both sides of him and though he peered and craned about, he could see no way of getting out from under its weight. He tried scratches and hoof traces to mark its stages yet there was no gain in this either for later he often found them already ahead of him.

It was as his head lay dragging on the pebble grit that suddenly there was a black part stoppering the roundness. He snap-snapped with his jaw and began snouting towards it. And then the scent was there too, heavy and close, and immediately he rose right up with a violence of rut noises and his yard thrusting out vigorously before him. Fierce shooting sliced in his head but he just brushed at it and sprang forward to break his way in from the roundness.

Slowly the troating gave out in him and its end sounds settled away in the distance. Now, in the quiet, his head was rocking and his eyes toppling back as he looked up at the great whiteness falling from high under the light. Downwards it spread, doubling out in its folds and overlayers, hanging far and loosely into lightness and then further again among the inner edges of the dark. And he saw, saw too how all of its falling was from her, high up, whiter yet of face and so still, with her berried lips and her hair that was long in its fairness.

He stayed and was swaying for suddenly it was her and words of what she had always been were upon him and he

166

was hearing them already in a greeting of honour. In his joy, his mouth opened to speak them out loud but instead there came bursting sounds of the rut. And straightaway with that, the dark was moving towards him with jostles of noise but then was slipping back below with everywhere about becoming white to his hocks in airy floatings of nothingness. And he went, trampling up into it, feeling height and rumours of space growing on his flanks till, far up, his head bent back to speak powers on the air and light falling threw his vastness of horn shadow upon her.

Mantling softness scattered beneath him as he rode up on to her. Rowan-red only were her mouth and the edges of the crescent in her thighs; complete white of moon, she lay lulled among the padding of hoofs for wonders of her own were deep in the blueness of her eyes. Yet he saw and did not see for there was only the heat of him between the coolness and it was touching against what was soft and now was pressing at the parting and suddenly all the weight of his rut was there on the brink of her; and even as he went, he felt himself being drawn in and sleekly and so too it seemed the fleet of a smile passed on her face. And at that, breath pinched off in him for deep chill inside her was about his yard; but already the rut driving was on him and his haunches were plunging in the juice of her suppleness.

I am the fear and the force. I am the stronghold of the dark. I gave suckling and lay with you in the needs of the earth and your despair. I was the guardian of belief, the pathway of all knowing, the speaking in the night. I have been the wellspring of your words; I have been the grieving and the joy. Yours I have been but mine you always were . . .

The words went dizzying about him and his teeth ground at the wonder of them for now joy of his truth seemed closing close with the speedings of his body. Elsewhere, suddenly, there was something dark and unbearable; but with the words purling around him, the knot of warmth was growing, gathering tauter so that his haunches came slowing into enormous strokes and a stillness settled on the crownwork of his head.

And dragged through from deep inside, the pulsing broke free with suddenly the dark in his head swelling beyond all bounds and then his tightness was clenching, clenching, clenching into looseness and even as it was, from out of the mass of dark, an awl of pain came striking at the back of his eye.

Seed bursting shuddered on under him as his head racked back on a neck set as stone. And his cry, wailing high, soared out into silence.

. . . but mine you always were.

Kuno was running and the sun was resting on the trees.

At the ground, his words only told them what they had all but known; yet cries went up as the fullness of horror broke upon them. But quickly now he set them to put dousing on the fire and then, laden with their dread, they made on down to the Scaur.

There he turned to them.

'Tomorrow, early,' he said, 'we shall hunt a buck of the first head.'

'But, Kuno, it is the close month!' they replied.

'It must be done nevertheless,' he answered. 'It is a way of old for times of such need.'

As the day went out, they set a fire to burn for their safekeeping and it was for Gort as the youngest to see it through the night. But long after they had left him and with quiet lying still under the stars, he suddenly sat up, jolted alert from his dozing by the flames. And as he turned, a swiftness of the air came upon him so that his head jumped clear of his shoulders and went rolling in the dust.

'Our rewards come to us all by and by,' said Bobba, wiping the sword.

By the gateway, the dogs had bolted the deadly food and were already beginning to falter about and slink for cover. Passing down among them, Bobba went to the barriers and quickly set himself to work. Balk and pale he had put aside and was just cutting at the thongs when flicker of light showed up beyond and feet were there.

Noiselessly, he began to draw open the gate. But even as he did, it burst breaking back on him and the women in their masses came forcing in. Oiled over and fearless with frenzy, they surged past and went crowding on towards the huts. Bobba, standing back, then slipped out for the gate; but a pack of them turned and fell on him, dragging him up by the hair.

'The boat!' they howled into his face.

And he could only make mumblings to them, saying this and that of what came into his head. But they were full of dark laughter and one of them tore out his eyes before they strangled him and threw his body on the fire.

Now light was growing as trees of flame went up from the huts. In the bevies of sparks worming above, birds of the night crazed here and there; and shouts were rising with them as the women crushed and milled and were ready for their chance. Away on one side, with her arms folded, stood the woman with the white sow's head.

One of the doors burst its barring and men came spinning out naked on the back of the smoke rush. Edge of weapon wielded into the host sent women lopped and stumbling; but always others were there and tooth and scoring nail were soon past the blades and bearing the bodies down.

Round behind, beneath dark sheerness of rock, the wall of a hut shook and shivered apart under axework. Out of the smoke came Ansi and Kuno too, followed by Leudi. Kuno seized up the axe and was making out into the screams and light when Leudi put his strength of hold on him. Tears came to his eyes as he shook his head. And indeed, at that very moment, the uproar billowed up with bayings as the women ran in, vying for what somewhere had been caught.

Passing beneath the pines, the three moved pale among shadows towards the entranceway. As the great hut's roof cracked folding in and the sky brightened out over the Scaur, they went silently down the slope and so on into the open night.

Later, as they came up by a distant crest, they caught sight of the Scaur once more. Fires burning there seemed mere wavers now: for down below in the summer forest, squalling fists of flame were lined out and building into a raking wall among the trees.

It was as the Tineman and his men passed on beyond and over the ridge that the moon began to rise full into the southern sky.